I0548332

Blinded by Shadows

A Working Man's Diary

by

Victor Anthony

"Those in the darkness have no need for light; for it will only blind their shadows." - Anonymous

1   ©2015

It was always my Dad against me, the least versus the most. I was the one who earned his ire merely by existing. I was the opposite of what was "right" in his mind. I'm not going to have to keep taking this...... his disapproving looks, the self-satisfied pat on the head of his beloved dogs. The dogs that always seemed to receive in excess everything I lacked. Despite my begging, my longing.... they received it all...approval, affection, encouragement...without even asking for it.

What is fair and what is not really doesn't matter...I have been made to pay. My twin brother never had to ask for a damn thing. He apparently was deserving, worthy in a way I couldn't conceive or understand. That was made clear....he was like those dogs, automatically included no matter what, because he had landed on the right side of Dad's judgment. HE was always one of the people that my Dad decided were good enough for his standards. My Dad held him up as the template of what I should be...of how success as his son was defined. On the inside of our house, it was like a laboratory. My brother and I were the rats, running the maze of his behavioral experiments, his constant tests of our abilities and whether we measured up.

©2015

My brother and the dogs were apparently fit to bask in the glow of Dad's success and receive its warmth with no conditions.... they were not made to suffer through brow-beating silence and unending strings attached to every gesture of parental kindness large or small.

It's not as though I have had it the bad per se... there are others much worse off than me. I went to the right schools, I have a professional degree. I tried to become what he expected...but its hard to strike a moving target...and much easier to become one. In the beginning, I tried very hard to become the opposite of what he had already decided I was from the beginning....a disappointment...a problem...the bad twin.

Haven't I put up with enough? His constant jabs, his withholding of everything that may signal a shred of closeness, of kindness to me? I have learned what type of world this is...of what it can be. Cruelty is an accepted norm that sometimes takes place quietly, insistently, in the smallest of unrelenting ways that gradually add up to an inevitable crushing burden.

©2015

*I am tired of this burden...so unbelievably tired......
it is time for someone else to take this burden
from me. I know that I can find someone that is
deserving of the task.*

©2015

Day 1 – I sit in my tiny bedroom office, surrounded by the shabbiest of items as I try to eke out an existence in the wake of the largest financial crash in 70 years. There was no denying that the pressure was on, that my family's well-being hung in the balance as I made every effort to move forward and make something from almost nothing. However, events were beyond my control, and success, if it could even be called that, was measured in the smallest of ways.

Projects completed here...a couple of dollars in the door there. A new idea fleshed out...a new skill learned. Unfortunately, none of those things replaced the six figure income I had lost nearly 3 years before, and the bitter end of my dwindling financial rope was in sight. A number of unfortunate outcomes needed to be considered, to be reckoned with....

As I sat in my tiny room this day, my cell "office phone" rang. It was an old co-worker of mine.

I had been on countless interviews...phone interview, first round in-person, second round in-person, final round office walk-around. I had filled out over 300 job applications. I had taken innumerable mind-numbing personality tests that I knew would screen me out of the job I was

©2015

applying for before I even answered the first question. Mine was never a personality easily categorized and boxed into a data point...and in this environment that could be a major detriment.

The co-worker who called was Mitch Berg, whom I had worked with periodically a few times over the last several years. Mitch was a decent enough guy I suppose. Unusual is perhaps a better, or more generous, term. I was never quite sure where he was coming from and he seemed to make the most awkward comments he could any time you spoke to him for more than 5 minutes.

"Hi Chris this is Mitch Berg calling how are you?" The formality and stiffness of his tone suggested that I hadn't known him for almost 6 years.

"Good Mitch, how are you?" I didn't respond in kind with the same formal tone, as it seemed like a strange and useless charade to act like I didn't know someone.

"I'm calling because I wanted to see if you might know anyone for a job that I have available. It is really sort of an entry level job, probably not something that you would be interested in, but I thought you might know someone."

 ©2015

Of course, Mitch knew that he was talking to someone who hadn't been in a formal, paycheck job for the better part of 3 years from emails we had exchanged over the last 15 months or so. He also knew I had a family. However, he kept up with what appeared to be a sort of "test commentary" to see how I would react.

"Yes Mitch, I know someone....I would be interested in the position depending on what it was." I said.

"It's really more of phone pounding-type position where I am working at, so I know you've said that you didn't want to do that anymore...and this is a new division that I am just starting up" Berg said, a little pride and boastfulness leaking out of his voice.

"Mitch, I've been out of work for a long time, if the opportunity is good and real, I would certainly consider it. Other than that, I can't say I really know anyone...."

"It's really more for a young guy who is looking to pound the phones and make some money..." This little bit was delivered matter-of-factly, as if there was someone who actually made it their life's goal from childhood to grow up, go to college, get out

©2015

of school and pound cold calls to people who hate you for 8 hours a day. Not that such a job was a means to an end...but that it was the end, a career destination in itself.

I began to wonder what the point of the call was, because he continued talking a long time after I told him that I didn't know anyone and he kept insisting it wasn't the right fit for me. He explained that the position was at a division of a larger public company and not a true "start-up", and that it had good benefits.

He finished with saying... "It's probably not really for a senior guy like yourself". There was a hint of condescension and gloating in his voice.

"Well Mitch, I guess it's not for me if you say so, but I don't know anyone" I decided to call his bluff, not really understanding what his point was in the first place.

He replied. "I didn't say it wasn't for you, I just wanted you to understand that it wasn't going to be the type of money you were used to before...."

"Mitch, I've been out of work a long time, so if the opportunity is real and the company is good, I am interested...." It was very hard to tell who was trying to convince whom at this point, as he had

8   ©2015

seemed to waver back and forth in his own mind. It was as though he only wanted me to be interested if I became convinced that he didn't think I was right for the position. Once I began believing his story...he seemed satisfied for some reason.

He replied "Ok fine, let me see what I can do....I just want you know that there are no guarantees or promises, and I will be back in touch with you."

No guarantees was a concept that coiled around me each day like bubble wrap, slowly suffocating my will to move on...to keep trying.....to not give up.

Day 30 - I got a call two days ago from Mitch indicating he wanted to have dinner to discuss the potential position with me. This evening we decided to meet up in the city. Berg, who had declared himself the restaurant authority, had decided where we were going to meet. It was someplace in the West Village that he insisted had a great reputation. I, being the one looking for a job, did the best I could to sound cheerful in agreeing to this, even though I knew the trip into the city would be an expensive one. On the way

©2015

in, I encountered heavy traffic at the Holland tunnel, and called Mitch to let him know I would be late.

"Mitch, it's Chris, I just wanted to let you know that I hit some heavy traffic at the Holland tunnel"

"What do you mean?" his abrasive tone indicating irritation. There was crowd noise in the background.

I thought my statement to him seemed fairly straightforward, but my distant memory led me to believe this type of reaction might not be unusual for Mitch as it first appeared. Paranoia was a big part of Mitch's makeup from what I remembered about our previous work experience together.

"Yeah...I'm sorry, I guess I left too late and I didn't really think there would be this much traffic going into Manhattan from Jersey at 7p at night. But I am on my way."

There was a brief pause of silence in which I could almost hear the wheels turning in his mind on the other end.

"Um, Ok, so exactly where are you right now?" Berg said, the trepidation in his voice noticeable.

 ©2015

"Trapped in a big lineup at the tunnel, waiting to go through the toll booths. I should be there but I'll probably be around 45 minutes late. My apologies."

There was a brief moment of silence, then Mitch spoke up.

"Oh..well, I guess I'm going to have make some new friends. Don't be surprised if I'm drinking my way through the next hour or so."

My recollection of Mitch was that he would talk to anyone, so I didn't fully grasp why he was having an issue with this relatively minor scheduling hiccup now.

"Sure, I understand. Sounds like fun." I said.

"I'm not sure FUN is the word that I would use, but I guess I have no other choice. Wait....so when did you say you would be here again?" he asked impatiently.

"Um...let me see...it's about 7:30 now. I shouldn't be any later than 8:30 tops." I said.

"Wait, I thought you said you were at the Holland tunnel, that means you should be here in no more

                    ©2015

than a half hour or 45 minutes. Why would it take you so long?"

Now he was really starting to get more than a little irritating. This was a simple courtesy call that was rapidly devolving into some type of debate.

"Yeah, well I suppose you are right, but given the way it's gone so far, I would say 8:30 would be the latest I would get there, who knows it may go quicker but I still have to park and make it to the restaurant. Parking isn't easy in the West Village."

"Oh yeah, it'll be no problem, you'll be here by 8p. I can tell you a great garage to park in that will get you here real quick. You have the address to the restaurant right?"

I now felt as though I was being tested. I also wasn't sure how a 'great garage' would get me there any quicker given the fact that once you are at the garage, you presumably had already made it through the worst of any traffic.

"Yep, it's in my pocket."

"What is it?" Berg said, firing this off quickly before the sound of my words had even fully

©2015

completed the journey through the phone and into his ears.

"I don't have it in front of me but I have the address, don't worry."

Another brief few seconds of silence.

"Ok great, do you want the location of that garage? It's super easy to get to and right across the street from the restaurant."

This last bit was a thinly veiled command masking as a courtesy. I was beginning to feel uncomfortable with the tone of the conversation, as well as its length while I was trying to negotiate traffic. I didn't appreciate the insinuation that I was lying to him and what seemed like a lack of belief he had in me for some reason I didn't understand. I had never stood him up or lied to him in the past, yet I felt as though I was being given the third degree for no apparent reason.

Now I had to answer as to why I didn't want to park in a garage when I thought the answer should be readily apparent to anyone who has ever been unemployed in NYC for any length of time, as I knew he had.

 ©2015

"Mitch, I'm not really looking to park in a garage because it's pretty expensive and I got to watch my money given my situation."

"Oooh yeah. Ok. Right. Alright well do the best you can and I will see when you get here. Give me another call if anything else comes up ok?"

I guess this meant I was off the hook for now...

"Yep, will do. See you in about an hour." Berg said.

"Yep see you in about 30 minutes then. Bye"

Wow. He just moved up my schedule another 30 minutes, at least as far as he was concerned. I knew there was little chance I would make that deadline, but I at least tried to reassure myself that it was given to me, rather than me telling him.

I wasn't sure what was more of a chore, the conversation I just had with Mitch or contending with the immense traffic jam going into the tunnel. I suddenly found myself remembering in more detail what an odd duck he really was. It could very well be a long night, but I had to find a way to get through it.

14   ©2015

After almost an hour I found a street spot that barely fit my car and made my way the two blocks to the restaurant.

When I arrived, Berg was clearly a bit drunk and talking very loudly to a middle aged couple he had apparently befriended in my absence.

"Oooh OK so you are from Finland. I see. I was confusing Sweden and Finland. So what do you think of the food in New York as compared to Sweden?" Mitch said to them.

They both looked at him rather quizzically, and the wife said something to her husband in Finnish.

"We are from Finland, and we have been to New York many times and always love the restaurants here." The grey haired husband stated matter-of-factly.

As I moved into Berg's field of vision, his face lit up and his voice rose what seemed like another three octaves. Meanwhile, crowds swirled around us in a very busy dining room that was as loud as a football stadium.

"Heeeey Chris, great to see you!!! You finally made it! I was just about to call you again. My good buddy Chris, woooow! Great to see you! I

 ©2015

want to introduce you to my new friends that I've been chatting with. This is Leo and Sara....um...ahh...how do I say. ooomkayla???"

They both looked at him and then at each other, barely suppressing smiles.

"Umkala"

"Oh yeah...right...right....Yumkahtla. Please forgive me, the last time I had to speak Swedish was when I watched the Swedish chef on the Muppet show!"

Berg than made a funny face that was intended to be humorous but really just made everyone feel uncomfortable as hell.

Both Mr. & Mrs. Umkala by now had just blank expressions on their face while they stared at Mitch and said nothing. I meanwhile sat next to him, praying that this diatribe was my imagination and not really happening.

"So Chris, Leo and Sara were just telling me about how they travel here all the time. Leo works for an accounting firm and Sara is a homemaker. Well, its been a pleasure speaking to you but my good buddy Chris is here and we're going to order now."

©2015

He then awkwardly shook both of their hands and made a stiff gesture to excuse himself.

Why he kept referring to me as "his good buddy Chris" was strange. I hadn't seen him in 3 years. Because the restaurant Berg had chosen featured communal style eating, the tables were essentially long picnic style and there was little separation from the people who were not in your party. This, along with the general confusion and the crowds caused everyone to talk loudly, and caused Mitch to basically be screaming. He couldn't have weighed more than 135 pounds and had also had several drinks, so being buzzed was really amping up his normally loud high pitched nasal voice even louder.

"(throat clear) Sooo, you finally made it. That traffic jam must have really been bad!"

Well, yes, I had called to tell him that.

"Yep, it was. Huge backup on the Jersey City side going into the tunnel."

"Wooow. Thats really weird for a Tuesday night. Usually not a big night in the city" he said.

"Well, it looked like there was some type of accident as I saw flashing lights at the tunnel."

"Really?! That's weird because I checked 1010 WINS right after I talked to you and they didn't say anything.(long pause with a quick head twitch) Oh well, whatever your reason for being late was, it really doesn't matter because you are finally here."

I felt a flash of anger pass through me as I got the distinct impression that Berg was insinuating I was a liar. At the same time, his saccharin attempt at making it seem as though it was no big deal made me even more upset. I now was in the uncomfortable position of having to defend myself for something I didn't do, or ignoring the comment completely because at the end of the day, he knew I needed his help and he knew I needed this job. I then began to think that he was just toying with me because he knew that he could, that he had the advantage.

Despite my low-key furor, I chose to say nothing and change the topic.

"So what time did you get here.?" I asked.

It was now 8:40 pm.

"I got here about 7p when YOU told me you'd be here!" Berg said in an mildly accusatory tone.

18   ©2015

"Right, well as we just discussed…." I began to say.

Mitch immediately cut me off with a rapid fire splatter of words.

"(throat clear)…I know I know…I'm just kidding. You don't have to get all upset. It was actually fine because I got to enjoy some great drinks and met some really great new friends while I was waiting for you to show up. Plus now I get to hang out with my good buddy Chris!"

To say that the Finnish couple were great "new friends" seemed like a bit of a stretch, as I got the distinct impression that they were more than a little freaked out by his presence and non-stop monologging about God knows what while they tried to have dinner as a couple. It sort of seemed like Mitch had attached himself to them.

The menus were delivered and I chose to keep my mouth shut while I looked it over, silently wondering what Mitch Berg's deal was. I had never been to dinner with him and this was already shaping up to be a strange evening.

"This is one of my favorite restaurants in the Village, Sevilla. I used to go here with my ex-

 ©2015

girlfriend all the time. You should try their steamed mussels. They are excellent."

"I'm not a huge seafood fan but I'll check it out" I said, probably releasing more truth than I should have.

"Reaaally? Wow. I didn't know that. Everybody likes seafood that I know. I figured coming from Chicago you'd be a big seafood fan!"

How those two things got put together in Mitch's mind I have no idea as Chicago was not exactly on the coast or known for its seafood. Lake Michigan was big, and there were certainly those who swore by Lake Perch and a few other freshwater varieties, but in my experience Chicago hadn't been known as a seafood destination for anybody.

"So were you a big fan of The Fridge and all those guys from the Bears?"

"Ah, yeah, well back in high school that was a lot of fun..." I said weakly.

The fact that the Bears players he was talking about hadn't played in 25 years didn't seem to even be recognized to him. He spoke about them as though they were on the cover of Sports Illustrated just last month.

 ©2015

"Growing up I was always talking about the Jets. Never could get into the Giants." Mitch offered.

"Yeah, the Jets were and still are a hard luck team for sure, a little like the Chicago Cubs. Never could get over the hump."

Berg cut me off and immediately spat out his next sentence with a stone cold look on his face.

"I didn't say I was a Jets fan per se. It was just that people all around me growing up always talked about them. I'm more of a Redskins fan!"

"Oh really, I didn't know you grew up in Washington, I thought you went to college there."

"Yes, I did. I got into the Redskins when I was in college at GW." Berg said.

The fact that none of this really made sense seemed to be lost on him, and I found talking to him to be some kind of low-grade skirmish that never resulted in anything satisfying. Clearly, there was no way he could have been a Redskins fan as a kid if he didn't even become one until college. Nevertheless, this is what he was insisting. And he was insisting it in a very pointed way, as though his life depended on me buying this story as true.

 ©2015

"Oh, ok. So you were a Jets fan growing up?"

"No, no. A lot of people around me were." Berg offered as though this was patently obvious and I was dense for not understanding it implicitly. I dropped the topic as a dead end and proceeded to something I thought would be a less contentious path.

"So how did you find out about this place?" I asked.

"You've never heard of it? Wow. This is one of the most well known restaurants in this part of the West Village. I can't believe you haven't ever been here. How long have you been in New York, like 10 years now?"

"Yep, about 10 years."

"Woooow. to think we've worked together twice over that time. You know if you end up getting this job that will be two jobs that I've gotten you."

I guess I was supposed to feel inadequate for two types of ineptitude at this point. One for my culinary ignorance and the other for my inability to be employed without the helping hand of Mitch Berg.

   ©2015

Berg continued.

"Ya know, I just think that it's real important to do a Mitzvah. Do you know what a Mitzvah is? It's something I grew up with that my parents always taught me. If you can help out another person, do something good, you should. So I thought I would do a Mitzvah. So now you really owe me! Heeeey... I'm just kidding. Anything for my good buddy Chris!"

I sat and took my medicine that was being doled out by Mitch in heaping gobs.

"So have you decided what you are getting? I wonder if this place has Whiskey? I've been going to a lot of Whiskey tastings lately and it is really fascinating. I had no idea that there was so much to learn!" he continued.

At that point the waiter arrived and we decided to order. After about an hour we finished. The bill was placed on the table by the waiter. Mitch immediately began examining it as though it was the secret formula for the cure to cancer.

"Ok, so you had more drinks than me and your entree was more expensive. The bill is 100 bucks, but I'll cut you some slack, just pay me 50 and

    ©2015

we'll call it even. I'll even pick up the tip." Berg said.

"Mitch, that's really not necessary, just let me know what my portion of the bill is and I'll pay it. Let me see the bill." I said, not wanting to play the "bill" game on this particular evening.

"No, no no....I got this. I know you've had some tough times and I've been there too buddy! We'll just call it even and when we go out for a few drinks after this you can pick up the first round. Not a problem for my good buddy Chris! That's what friends are for right?" Mitch said.

I'm not sure if he was gloating or he was trying to insult me, or maybe he thought that this was some type of gesture, but the net effect was that it was annoying as hell. However, I held my tongue and kept my focus on doing what I had to do to get the job.

After the bill was paid we stepped out onto 8th Avenue and began walking North.

"Isn't the Chelsea hotel up here?" I said. I had always had a big of a fascination with the place as the former home of favorite writers and musicians. I had been to the bar on the ground floor several years before.

24 ©2015

"Yeah I think so." Mitch said.

"That's it.......we have to go." I said.

It appeared that Mitch was game as he didn't appear to have any ready alternative choice lined up. We turned on 23rd street and soon arrived at the old hotel, peeking into its Lobby before stepping into the adjoining restaurant and Bar. We had been together for two hours and he still hadn't said a word about the position, so I was hoping that our time here would be what I actually came for. I didn't want to seem greedy or ungracious, but I was starting to wonder what was going on.

Otherwise, this would be just another long-winded exercise in futility.

Finally, we settled into the bar and Mitch, who ordered some type of exotic and expensive whiskey that I would be paying for, began talking.

"So, how bad do you need a job?" Mitch opened up.

"Pretty bad, that's why I am here...." I offered, stating what I thought seemed obvious by now.

"So you need one really bad?"

 ©2015

"Yes Mitch, I definitely do. What, you don't believe me?" I said.

"No, I just wanted to see because this job is basically another one of these phone pounding type sales positions, and you said to me several times when you got promoted at Direct Max that you wanted to branch out into other things and that phone pounding was something you didn't do anymore. Of course the ironic part was that you ended up training the phone pounders there, which was kinda funny don't ya think? Remember that time you trained me? Anyway, the culture at this place is a lot different than what I am used to....nobody works! I leave there at 6p or later every night and I am the only person left. During the day the office is quiet as a library and I often sit there and ask myself "what are these people doing?'. It is a total corporate, big company type of setup but at least they pay a base salary and good benefits. I was hired as the first salesperson because my boss Steve couldn't sell and basically nobody else that tried to sell there could do it either. Of course the first month I was there I closed like 20 deals and the President of the company, who happens to work in our office came by my desk and said to keep up the good work. I don't know what was so hard, it just a matter of

  ©2015

being productive and working. So anyway, I guess they really like me there…..."

This speech went on for what seemed to be at least another 10 minutes as I found myself trying to not only understand him, but keep a look on my face that indicated interest.

Finally at the end of this, Mitch said.

"So do you still want the job?"

"Yes, this totally seems like something that I could do. Sounds familiar and sorta similar to what we did at Direct max."

"OK great, but I'm going to warn you that my boss can be a little strange sometimes. He likes to bust balls and he and I have a great working relationship together but he might lay into you a little because you are the new guy."

"I'm pretty sure I can handle it Mitch, it wouldn't be the first time, but thanks for the heads up."

"Like I said, he and I get along great, so it will be a shoe in for you to get the interview. As long as you have my recommendation you are as good as in."

"Ok great Mitch, I really appreciate it" I said.

     ©2015

With that, we finished our drinks and ambled back to my car. I offered to give him a ride uptown so he could make his way to the east side without having to take a crosstown bus or cab.

After dropping him off, I reflected on what a strange evening it had been, and how getting through it, while made easier by a few drinks, was more of a chore than a pleasure. However, I had to keep my focus on the only thing that mattered, making sure I got the job so I could start digging out from the very deep hole I found myself in. My family's future depended on it.

Day 44 – After the crash of 08 and perhaps for a long time after, the search for work was often a demeaning round robin of callbacks that never came, phony and upbeat assessments that meant little, idiotic personality tests, and rounds of interviews that could number into the double digits before an offer, or more likely, a non-callback, was forthcoming. The internet had brought lying, half truths, and deception to a new level of proficiency for companies that knew they had 500 applicants for every job, no matter what the pay or responsibilities were.

   ©2015

In between was the waiting. This yawning space of time that was always looking to be filled, and needed to be kept topped off with something resembling positive and productive activity.

It was against this backdrop that I received a call from Mitch's boss, Steve Klein.

"Hello this is Chris." I answered.

A voice came on the other line that sounded professional and calm.

"Hello Chris, this is Steve Klein with Sharetech, Mitch works with me and referred you over as a potential candidate for the position here in our Recovery group. How are you today?"

I won't bore you with the rest of the details of this largely rote conversation, I'll only tell you the end result was that I was to go on an interview with Steve in a week's time, the early part of December. What I knew by the end of the conversation was that the job had potential, even if it was a "step down".

What "step down" meant after almost 30 months of being out of work was of dubious value anyway. All steps had been down for a long time, and any future experience that I was comparing to the past

     ©2015

as some type of career move was questionable at best. This was about survival pure and simple. Success had been re-defined as not ending up in foreclosure and having my kids taken and my wife leaving me. The three car garage, corner office, and trips to Europe were things that took place in some alternate reality that existed in a dimension far from my own.

The position we discussed on the phone appeared to play to my strengths as a start-up, boot strap guy, without all the risk of having to work purely on your own. Sharetech was a large multi-national corporation looking to expand into new areas of revenue. A big part of my job would be to help make that happen.

The first order of business would be to knock down some doors and bring in the initial sales for the division, along with Mitch and Jim Azov, another guy I had known at a previous job along with Mitch. The salary wasn't great, but it was a big improvement over my current predicament and the big-company benefits were sorely needed for my family. At best, we would be the heroes of a new successful division. At worst, I could eke out a few more years of survival and get the kids healthcare up to date.

   ©2015

Day 51- Interview Day- The journey into lower Manhattan was a strange revelation. I had worked there several times in the past 12 years, but it had been awhile since I had made the journey. It was a sense of fanciful dislocation...somewhat like being resurrected after being in some type of purgatory-like cocoon in my bedroom office for three years.

I was good at acting like I knew what I was doing, and I drew heavily on these skills as I made my way to the high-rise on Water Street near the Seaport in lower Manhattan.

I went through the front door and moved into the marble lobby to the doorman and announced myself. Within a few minutes, Mitch had come down to meet me, embracing my hand in a highly tense simulation of a genuine greeting. He then informed me that the person who was my potential boss, Steve Klein, would be down in a few minutes.

The intervening time was spent showing me around the office. The office "tour" was a routine I knew well at this point, and I had been shown my prospective cubicle on many previous interviews that never seemed to pan out. The view of the Brooklyn Bridge was spectacular, but I reminded

    ©2015

myself not to get taken in by it...and I didn't dare envision myself here. That just wasn't healthy.

Mitch left for a few moments after the tour and told me to wait in the floor's reception area. Upon his return, he told me to head downstairs to the Café Europa that was in the lobby and that Steve would meet me there.

I did as I was instructed, no longer nervous or even anxious. This had become a routine with a predictable script, and my job was to read my lines convincingly...to do a good job, but not too good a job....to act confident, but not so confident that my potential boss might feel threatened. This was how the game was played...and after many turns of the wheel, I understood perfectly what was required....or so I thought.

I bought a coffee in the Café and waited, careful to get the smallest size due to my dwindling funds, and it occurred to me that I didn't know exactly who I was looking for. I had no idea of his appearance....only his name. However, even this scenario had played out many times before...and somehow two expectant people who are looking about usually seem to find who they are looking for.

32 ©2015

Steve came in, dressed in a conservative Navy blue suit. He was of average height, and had thinning salty black hair. He was perhaps 50 years old. The greeting seemed normal enough as he sat down at my table.

"I'm Steve Klein from Sharetech; I understand you know Mitch Berg?"

"Yes we worked together at a previous job, Direct Max Inc., you may have noticed it on my resume."

He began to shuffle through the resume, but like most interviewers, comprehended maybe 2 percent of what was on it. I'd often thought that since the dawn of the internet, I should just create a resume full of 20 key words in bold typeface, because usually that was all people saw anyway. The rest you had to explain in an interview because the person interviewing you usually had done exactly 30 seconds of preparation before they met you.

"So...how well do you know Berg?"

Mitch apparently held the title of sales manager from what I had been told to this point, with Steve being the Vice President in charge of the division. It seemed rather strange that he was already calling his sales manager by his last name less than

   ©2015

2 minutes after meeting a prospective job candidate.

"Well, we worked together several years ago at Direct Max and then again at a different job back in 2008. Other than that I had only seen him when we had dinner to discuss this job a few weeks ago."

"Oh yeah...did you know he actually tried to expense that dinner to the company?" Klein asked.

Ok...now this was officially getting strange...but I had to roll with it. I needed the job. It was times like these that I held my tongue and tried to think only about my children.

"Really, I had no idea...he didn't mention that." I offered.

I genuinely was surprised as Mitch had never made any mention of this, and the way the dinner had played out at the time it appeared completely like a personal expense, especially because I had paid for my half, and the large drink bill afterwards.

"Yeah...I totally didn't authorize him doing that." Klein said flatly.

©2015

"Strange, because I actually believe that I paid for my half of it" I said.

It was true that I was taken aback...and for some reason a bit offended. I suppose it was because Mitch hadn't mentioned expensing it at all and had made such a show of being "my good friend" and kept saying rather uncomfortably "my good buddy Chris" while we had dinner. It actually got to the point where it was weird. This confirmed in my mind that it really was all for my benefit, a show perhaps, that only mattered to him.

"Typical Berg....always trying to cheap out the company" Steve said.

This last line that was put forward by Klein in a juvenile and mocking imitation of Mitch's high pitched nasal voice, along with an attempt at a weird face.

For a guy who thought he had seen everything, this was new....the superior of your potential boss doing disrespectful imitations of him during the interview process. Usually, there is at least a show of appearing unified to outsiders during this stage of the hiring process. The real deal normally shines through several weeks or months later, after it's too late.

 ©2015

Clearly, whatever respect Mitch thought he had at this job was non-existent. This was not entirely surprising, but I hadn't anticipated the extent of it this early in the process.

"Really? Yeah I guess so." I replied weakly, not really knowing where to go with this. It was a very strange position to be in. Klein continued...

"If you come onboard I just want you to know one thing, don't listen to Berg...he's gonna come up and tell you all this stuff...blah blah blah (Berg voice imitation) 'Ahhh Chris let me see your call reports" and this other stuff about counting calls and conversations. If any of that bothers you or he starts anything like that you come to me or my right hand man, Jim about it. I am the one in charge, not Mitch. I don't believe in watching over everyone like a hawk...if you do your job, you'll be fine, and I'm sure you will. If not, I'll know about it."

I couldn't help but crack a guilty smile. I mean this was ridiculous, wrong, and funny all at the same time. Clearly Mitch was completely hosed at this job. He had only been there 8 months and it was already close to open warfare between Steve and Mitch. Seething resentment was the phrase that came to mind.

©2015

"Ok I completely understand...I'll make sure I come to you." I said, sounding the part of a loyal soldier.

"So I am still waiting on the final word from global headquarters about whether we can hire you. I've been told that it is essentially a formality, but we still need final approval." Klein said.

"Any idea when you might hear?"

"I've been told soon, hopefully before the end of the year, but I will keep you posted. For some reason at this company they need to get approval from the CEO in Australia for this hire."

"Wow...OK" I said.

The interview ended there and I walked out onto Water Street, silently shaking my head to myself. It had been a strange interview to say the least. Nevertheless, I liked my chances. However, what Klein had said to me had made it very clear that battle lines were drawn. Namely, you aren't to be friends or seen to be 'on the side of' Berg. The undermining of Mitch Berg was already underway.

While I didn't agree with this, I was going to have to negotiate this particular workplace minefield very carefully if I did get hired. Luckily, I had

©2015

much experience at that task. I had a family, and I needed the job...and nothing could get in the way of that, including my own righteous sense of morality....there was no place for that in business, or in the role of provider that I currently found myself.

©2015

It sounds familiar now….very familiar. How he used to subtlety and skillfully undermine me. I was too young to notice what was going on, but I always felt its effects…the shame, the not measuring up…the naked inadequacy. It almost always surrounded something trivial with the dogs.

The goddamn dogs….they were like his litmus test. If you wanted to be part of what he was…..if you wanted acceptance, you needed to prove it through the dogs. Maybe it's because the dogs were always his most trusted advisers, the ones he truly needed. My mom was just serving a role, a function for him. Plus she was a woman, so really, how much value did her opinion have? He was a goddamn alpha male, captain of industry to be feared and respected….not a housewife.

I was supposed to walk the dogs, clean the dogs cage….speak to the dogs, play ball with the dogs. Whenever these orders came, I always tried, at least in the beginning, to do what was asked of me….but somehow…the dogs were never quite happy. He would swear this to me, up and down, that he could tell the dogs didn't like the way that I did it and then explain in excruciating detail how I had screwed up.

 ©2015

"See the way her ears are right now? That's because you scared her and she doesn't know how to handle what you are doing. Jesus...what the hell is your problem?" my Dad would say.

Yes...oh yes....those dogs had more nuances of emotion than any human ever could, according to him. And somehow when I was around they always reflected negatively on me. And the dogs were always by his side, unwitting companions in the little dramas that he cooked up in his head for me. I slowly came to hate them as symbols of what was wrong between us, which was pretty much everything. When I heard their names I would cringe, and half expect him to tell me that they had told him more things I had done wrong..and how my twin brother had done it better.

I remember when I got my first cat, many years later when I was in college.

At Thanksgiving, my father walked into my apartment and upon seeing my cat, kicked him as hard as could, sending him flying through the air with a screech of pain.

"What the fuck is a son of mine doing with a fucking cat?"

40   ©2015

Thanksgiving was a family time.

Thanks Dad.

©2015

Day 68 – First Day. I had injured myself and torn a muscle in my leg just before I got the call to start the job at Sharetech. Dancing with my kids was apparently a little too much fun. I hadn't gone to the doctor because we hadn't had health insurance for over 2 years, and there was no way I could afford it. I was getting better, but when the time came to go in on the first day, I was limping pretty badly, but still able to get around. Certainly, I wasn't going to miss the first day.

Once I got to the office and got upstairs, Klein, myself, and the other members of my group exchanged pleasantries. I was formally introduced to Jim Azov, the other sales person on the team besides myself and Berg. I soon learned they were considering hiring a fourth person, Omar Ahmedy, to round out the team.

I had also known Jim from a previous job where Mitch and myself had also worked. However, we had never worked this closely together. From what I knew of Jim, he always was an amiable guy and a good worker...easy to deal with if my memory served me correctly.

©2015

I was introduced around, and given the perfunctory HR once-over that goes on at every company. Then I stepped over to Klein's desk as I got settled in.

"So is that a limp you have or are you happy to see me?" Klein said.

"What?" I wasn't sure what he meant, but I had an idea.

"You know....it's so big....goes down your pant leg" He trailed off and raised his eyebrows with a shit eating grin.

Ok- so we were apparently doing dick jokes on my first day of work...not expected, but I wasn't ever going to give him, or anybody, the satisfaction of knowing that they had thrown me off.

"Of course it's big, I'm Italian." He seemed to like this....I was gonna play ball with his sick sense of humor.

"Not me....I'm Jewish" as if I was supposed to have understanding of what that meant in this context.

I really had nothing to say that would help my position so I instead changed the topic to something besides talking about our dicks.

 ©2015

Klein gave me a bit of standard speech about what we were doing and how the day went, and made mention of how Mitch would do some training. When mentioning this he barely concealed his mockery and disdain for the whole concept. It was as though letting Mitch hold the title of "sales manager" was just throwing him a meaningless bone, worth very little except he knew Mitch craved it. It was right about then that Mitch walked over, eager to insert himself into the situation.

He eagerly grasped my hand with an extreme amount of awkward tension.

"Heeeey Chris, its great to see you....welcome aboard!"

"Thanks Mitch...good to be here." I offered politely.

The whole thing seemed forced and phony, but no matter...I had a job. At least that's what I had to tell myself.

Mitch then proceeded to show me to my cubicle and began giving me various instructions on when tech would be by to give me my logins, getting office supplies, etc.

44   ©2015

Most of what he said was a rather confusing mash of words that I just nodded to while we he talked for what felt like 15 minutes straight. What I got out of it was that I couldn't do anything until I had gotten my logins from tech, so sit tight and tomorrow he would start some type of training with me.

What seemed strange to me was that it was clear there was a of charade of sorts going on between Klein and Berg. I knew from dinner out with Berg before I got the job that he was supposedly the "sales manager" in name, but had not received a raise or his "override". However he had started at a higher base salary than everyone else because he was the first hire.

Normally in the business world, an override means you were being paid money off the revenue other members of your team brought in as compensation for your leadership. Up until my hiring, that 'team' in our division at Sharetech included exactly one other person besides Mitch. Klein was the supervising VP so he didn't count in this calculation.

This, coupled with the fact that nature of the work were were doing meant we often didn't see revenue on our deals until years in the future,

©2015

made the concept of an override a tenuous one at best. But that didn't stop Berg, as he never let facts interfere with his version of reality. It's very hard to "get your override" when the revenue isn't booking for another two years.

It appeared Klein gave him this title as "manager" as a means to help induce Berg to take the job and start selling for the department and bring in new hires. Because Berg was older and had bounced around to many jobs previously, he was angling for authority and money in exchange for being the first hire of a new department. He also made it his life's mission to maintain contact with everyone he had ever worked with so he could call them up should he need them in a situation just like this. That tactic had worked with me quite well.

However, it seemed to me that Klein merely dangled this prospect of a manager title out in front of him, for Steve Klein had no actual authority, let alone intention, to ever give Berg the official title and salary raise that he so cravenly wanted and felt he deserved. It seemed that Berg had wheedled a promise out of him for these two things and that Klein sensed his desperate wanting and essentially "yes'd him" to death to get him in the door without ever

©2015

approving either item with upper management. Being an attorney, I'm sure Klein qualified those yes answers and never put them in writing, hoping that Berg wouldn't pay attention and take the job anyway.

Thus, the two were at loggerheads, and they both knew they needed each other for the time being, but each also saw the other as standing in the way of their progress. Given what I had seen so far of their personalities, it was a potent recipe for disaster.

Meanwhile, Jim Azov had been in the middle of these two for the last 6 months prior to my arrival. He definitely understood people well enough to know that there was potentially strength as well as risk in his position. While Berg was giving me his semi-incomprehensible "opening day new hire" speech, I looked over at Azov and saw him sitting at his cube rolling his eyes out of sight of Berg. I got the sense he was long suffering under the weight of both of them.

Right now, Azov was striking me as the most sane of the three, if for no other reason than he seemed to comprehend the utter foolishness of Klein's and Berg's behavior.

 ©2015

Before the end of the day, he had quietly sent me two emails that gave me a clear idea of how to begin doing my job....something that fifteen minutes of Berg's speaking had failed to do. It was basically a three sentence succinct translation of the lengthy talking that I had just listened to. I was grateful to have him helping me out.

The job itself was actually pretty simple, and it was taking me back to tasks that I had mastered years before, but now, in the wake of the collapse, was being called on to do again. It may not be ideal, but it could definitely work. Watching how all the people in department ended up trying to get along and work as a unit was going to be a much more difficult task. I had never seen so much potential conflict in such a short period of time. My plan at the outset was to try my best to stay above the fray and do my job so well that nobody in senior management would have an excuse to shut us down or fire me.

There was very little else that I could do for now. So I kept my head down and went about learning what I needed to do in order to make things happen.

©2015

Day 69- As part of my effort to be an effective employee, I put on a show about having a good attitude when training, even to myself. The truth was, as hidden as I tried to make it, I was grossly overqualified for the work. However, I was one of millions in that boat, so I would gladly eat my share of humble pie to retrieve a sense of normalcy for my family.

Because Berg was still clinging to the idea that he was the "sales manager", he had decided that all new employees needed training on how to make calls. It was clear to me that Klein was lukewarm to this idea at best, especially after listening to Berg on the phone, but he allowed it to occur solely to placate him for the time being.

Berg greeted me with his usual saccharin "charm", and told me we were going to do "some training" in a conference room.

"I hope you don't mind, it's just part of what we do when we bring a new hire on" Berg said.

I think this was meant to let me know I didn't really need it, but he had to do it anyway. Of course, I knew that wasn't true at all given Klein's attitude, but my goal was to play along for the

 ©2015

time being. Berg was seemingly on some type of mini power trip.

"Not a problem, I completely understand" I said.

"You did a lot training when we worked together before didn't you?" Berg said, already knowing that to be the case as we had discussed it many times over the years.

"Yeah, Mitch, you knew that" I had been the lead trainer for several hundred hires, including some of the people Mitch had hired to work with him at location he managed.

"That was a really big promotion for you back then wasn't it?" Mitch said.

I had told him this story at least half a dozen times in the past 6 years. It was the story of, at least as he heard it, how I got promoted and was successful and how he got promoted and then demoted and wasn't. However, he was a glutton for punishment, so apparently I was going to need to tell it again.

"I remember you actually trained me at one point." Mitch said in a particularly acid tone.

 ©2015

Mitch seemed to have trouble realizing that this wasn't a call center type job like our previous time working together had been. He was rigidly trying to take lessons from one job and bolt them onto another, regardless of whether it fit or made any sense.

We then went into a conference room where he shut the door and began the optimistically titled "training". We were going to start with some role playing, where I was the sales person and he was the prospect.

"Good morning, my name is Chris Matters from Recovery Resources…" I started.

"Ok stop there…do you really want to say your name first or do you want to announce why you are calling first and then say your name? It's totally up to you, but I'm just saying that I've had better success doing it that way. It can't hurt. Ok try again." Berg said.

"Good Morning, I'm calling from Recovery Resources regarding a potential refund that may be owed to your company from a recent settlement by the manufacturers of LCD flat panels…." I began again.

  ©2015

"Okay stop for a second....you do realize that your tone is really very low and you are speaking very fast right now? Remember, this is about having conversations with people, not about trying to just get your speech out there. We really want to engage....and what I like to do is really just speak conversationally with them and try and ask questions."

Berg was really starting to annoy me, as I started to feel that this training session was less about trying to do any actual learning and more about Berg grandstanding and listening to himself talk endlessly. The session continued.

"Mitch, I think that I am being conversational in my tone, do you really think it sounds that bad?" I was sure that it didn't but I had to play along like I was being cooperative and open minded.

"I didn't say it wasn't conversational at all. I didn't say that at all. I actually think you sound really good but, its also important to remember that we want to be having conversations with prospects, and not just pitching like robots."

"Mitch, I don't think I sound like a robot" I stated flatly.

©2015

"(throat clear) Heeeeeey...I'm not saying that at all. You sound greeaaat. I was just saying we want to be aware of that and make sure we are having conversations....why don't you start again from the top."

"Good morning, I'm calling from Recovery Resources..." I began again.

"Ok stop for a second, I like to actually say my name before I say the company name. I find that works best for me...I mean.... feel free to do it the way you want, I'm just saying it seems to make sense to announce who you are...."

"But Mitch, you told me a minute ago not to mention my name first..." I stated.

"Don't misunderstand me....I wasn't saying you shouldn't do it per se, what I was saying is there are times when that may not be the best route and other times that it is...it's really about the conversation and after all, it can't hurt..."

"So which way do you want me to do it?" I asked, getting impatient.

"Ah, well...I'm not here to tell you what to do, I just think that the most important thing to do is to be productive. And one of the ways to be

   ©2015

productive is to have conversations and introducing yourself can be, in some situations but not in others, a good way of doing that. On the other hand, you may feel that that it is less than ideal for you and that you might need to talk about the product first and what benefits it has for the prospect....I mean you know what you're doing, you don't need me to tell you this. You know what I mean?"

I had no idea what he meant.

He continued going on like this for the next 30 minutes, and I kept thinking back to what Klein had told me about not listening to a word he said. I found it to be the most confusing and annoying "training" session I think I had ever been a part of. It was more like some twisted type of Chinese water torture. Berg spoke incessantly, interrupting me after only a few seconds of "role play"...constantly contradicting himself and pretending to be friendly while doing it.

Then Klein stuck his head in.

"Berg, are you done yet?...You've been in here with him for an hour...." Klein looked at me rolling his eyes.

©2015

"Chris, you know what you're doing right?" I immediately nodded to Klein and looked over at Berg, who looked like somebody had just killed his pet rabbit.

As we both left the room, Berg said to me "Do you remember that time when we worked at DirectMax where I had to train with you?"

I had a vague recollection, but it was my job to train an awful lot of people, so I can't say I had a vivid memory of Mitch Berg in particular. I do remember that his main issue was that the length of his calls compared to his production was always a problem. In other words, he was not very efficient...but loved to talk, despite the fact he didn't sell much.

"Yeah sort of Mitch" I said.

"Boy I do...you were really hard on me." Mitch said.

Oh. Ok...so now I get it.

Apparently I had hurt his feelings 6 years ago and that is why I got "the business" from him today. In other words...payback. It sort of blew my mind that he had been harboring this for that long. That

©2015

was very hard core in a bizarre way.....and a little scary.

"I don't think I was hard on you...I was trying to help everyone get better...it was also my job to make sure people were capable of hitting the required metrics they were looking for back then."

"Well...you always were the 'tough love' guy...." Mitch offered, his phony upbeat tone barely masking his bitterness.

Um...ok...whatever that means Berg.

I found myself increasingly confused and annoyed by him as the days began to pass. His paranoia, insecurity, ego and anxiety were a constant source of irritation and he always seemed to find a way to make sure that It came out in an awkward and bizarre verbal exchange.

Day 76- Each day I find myself riding the train, convincing myself that I am thankful that I'm here, because that is what I should be...right?....... amongst these other stone-faced commuters and their smart phones. I remind myself that this is a great alternative to what came before...or maybe a more accurate statement is that it was the best

    ©2015

that could be hoped for right now. In my darker moments, I glance around the car in the morning and sometimes think that these ate all marked men and women.....waiting for the next spasm or downturn to thrust them off this train and into an uncertain future filled with an endless series of "what if's"........and then I chuckle to myself and my overactive imagination.

From my point of view, this wasn't a career so much as bloody fight for survival. There may not have been people who were physically destroyed, though there were a few....however, there were many that were damaged...some beyond repair. A career was having the wherewithal to get through the monotony and grind of the daily battle to grab a reward that might...or might not, lay on the other side.

The conductor clicked his clacker, reminding me to show my ticket. It then occurred to me that I had been staring out the window for the last 10 minutes.

Day 78- This past week Klein had told me to stop bringing new deals to Mitch for processing and logging in, and to bring them directly to him. My assumption was that this was one of many small moves intended to slowly remove as much power from Berg as he could, while still allowing him to retain the hollow title of "sales manager".

Oftentimes during the day, Berg, like a child who needs attention, would go over to Klein, who rarely rose from his cubicle, and begin asking him questions. Because I was within ear shot, and Berg talked incredibly loud, I could usually overhear that these were basic questions that he should either know, or were rather pointless to be asking. Klein would usually respond with some type of snide tone and throw the question back in his face.

If Berg was a cat, Klein was his toxic scratching post.

"So Steve, do you want us to log the new agreements into the V Drive under a separate folder and case name?" I heard Berg asking.

"What do you think?" Klein said to him, with just a hinted tone of sarcasm.

"Well, I was just asking because that is how we had always done it in the past, but I also know that we discussed this case the other day and I wasn't sure if this is how you wanted the team to

 ©2015

be handling this going forward for new cases and you and I hadn't discussed this before I messaged the protocol to the team so I just wanted to check with you and see if that was how you wanted to handle it." Berg blurted out nervously.

"Mitch, this is how we have always done it...the "team" can log their own deals and come to me individually, you don't need to put out one of your "team emails" or have one of your meetings. You just worry about your deals and let everyone else worry about theirs." Klein said impatiently.

Berg did not like this, because he perceived this as one of his precious "manager duties" and he took it as an affront that it had been so easily dismissed by Klein.

"Well I just figured that because I will be getting an override off of their production, I should be the one to convey and manage how they log new deals into the system." Berg said, his voice wavering and tense.

"First of all Mitch, the whole 'override' thing has not been approved, and I am not sure if it will ever be approved. When I mentioned this to Andrew, he acted like this wasn't something that

©2015

was done here....and he made no decision on it all." Klein said.

"What do you mean, I thought you said that they were discussing it?" Berg said, clearly peeved and nervous at the same time, unable to control his anxiety.

"Just what I said, there is no guarantee you are getting an override on everyone's production. You know how this company is...they are very tight with the dollar and don't really have a protocol for handling something like that. You are being paid a higher base salary than anyone else in the department. Don't forget that Mitch....."

However, by now Berg was visibly angry, and he stood next to Klein's cubicle ramrod straight, even though Klein was sitting down...as if girding for a fight or steeling himself as to whatever else might come out of his mouth next. He clearly didn't seem to be backing off.

"But I am the sales manager right? The sales manager usually gets an override." Berg said, as though this was a written law or one of the Ten Commandments. Perhaps he thought that if he said it again, it would be more likely to come true.

 ©2015

"Berg, there is no 'sales manager' position right now. I've told you that...and I told you that when you were hired. I told you that I would talk to them about it....just calm down until you hear from me." Klein said this with more than a little frustration, as if this conversation was one in a long string concerning the 'override'.

"It's not that I'm not calm. I am totally calm. I just wanted to know where I stand. It's not productive to be running every single deal directly through you as the VP. As the sales manager that should be my role...oh, excuse me, as the unofficial sales manager. I only say that because that's what you promised me when I was hired." Berg sounded jilted and bitter about this perceived injustice and he clearly didn't have a problem showing it.

"I think I can handle logging deals for now... because the sales reps do most of it themselves. All I have to do is countersign agreements. You guys are supposed to do the rest. I don't get the feeling from anyone that they are having trouble doing that on their own, so I'm not worried about productivity right now Mitch. Just make sure that you get your deals logged in correctly and we'll go from there."

   ©2015

At this, there was silence as Berg stalked away red-faced to his cubicle, feeling ever the more defeated by Klein. My co-worker Jim and I just looked at each other and tried to keep from rolling our eyes.

I sort of knew that this was vintage Mitch Berg, but I had never managed to see it this close-up or in such detail. He was completely tone deaf when it came to people, or understanding how to work with them when you didn't necessarily like or agree with them. His approach was one dimensional and unchanging...and Klein used this to his advantage when trying to aggravate him.

He and Klein were, in many ways, the perfect combustible mix for each other. It almost seemed that each of them saw something in the other that reminded them of themselves that they hated. Perhaps this aspect was something they were trying to avoid, and they channeled their resentment into each other at being forced to face it.

There was no lack of self-loathing going around between the two of them. And it was this realization that fueled their toxic back and forth dialog as the days passed. Oddly enough, it also seemed that they understood the power each had

      ©2015

over the other to get them emotional and upset….and they both clearly enjoyed this on some twisted level.

Meanwhile, the tension simmered underneath the surface as they both tried to figure out new ways to escalate the growing conflict that was becoming a battle of wills.

©2015

"Let me see that report card." my Dad said.

I knew that this was going to be another one of his meticulously drawn out fault finding sessions.

"I looked at your brothers...he is pulling a 4.0"

This was really just an implied threat, signaling the coming barrage of overt and subtle insults heading my way.

My grades, at least by the standards of many parents at that time, were never an issue in any sort of normal context. However, in my father's eyes, they were a disappointment that embarrassed not only him, but also my entire family, seemingly back several generations. It had been explained to me many times that this was a family of successful high achievers, and that I was surely going to fail his expectations in keeping this unbroken string of success going.

"You got a B in Trig? What the fuck is the problem?"

It hadn't mattered that I had struggled in that class or that I had gone for extra help, or even that I had asked him for help, in a futile attempt to make him understand. Despite all this, he acted completely dumbfounded, and of course

©2015

saw fit to bring my mother and my brother and sister into it so as to increase the level of pain and embarrassment for me.

"Eva, Jim, come over here...Steve got a B on his report card! Your brother got straight A's...with an A minus in gym. If you're going to go get a B and embarrass the hell out of me, why don't you do it in some class for losers like gym. You'll never do well in business if you can't do the math.....I've told you that a hundred times...but I guess listening is another skill that you are failing at this stage of your education. I got guys at my office who can do this sort of math in their head! And my own damn son looks at it like its some type of chore that he can't be bothered with."

In my Dad's world, being good with "the numbers" was tantamount to being a man. Only real men understood "the numbers", were good with "the numbers" and most importantly....on top of "the numbers". Always with the numbers, the deals, the projects...this is what he excelled at, and what he valued. Therefore, that was all that should matter for me as well.

The fact that these were all skills that he enjoyed and had a talent for seemed to escape him as he framed these skills to me as basic, essential and

©2015

unchanging truths of being "a man". Of course, the corollary to that was that he was always keeping score, as long as the score indicated that he was the "top man" in the room at any given time.

And the score, as far as it was concerned with me, his second twin son, wasn't in the winning column.

The day I came home from High School with a new Ramones album and blue streaks in my hair, my Dad looked at me with a mixture of disgust and disappointment, then turned away, muttering only one thing under his breath that was audible.

"Exactly what I expected from someone like you."

©2015

Day 86 – The weeks flowed on, and my work results were very encouraging. However, this took a back seat to what was rapidly becoming the most important thing produced in our department...the smoldering battle between Berg and Klein.

Berg had tried an escalating series of ham handed maneuvers to assert control in various ways. He would speak up in meetings and try and assert himself as the "manager", when clearly he wasn't able to see that nobody thought of him that way, least of all Klein. Additionally, many of his ideas were not good, were factually wrong and demonstrated a limited understanding of our product offering.

Klein would immediately pounce on this, at which point Berg would begin talking so fast that his words gave the impression of a rushing river, chaotic and incoherent. This would open Berg up to further attacks by Klein, who would usually attempt to bring Jim or myself to his side with him in the humiliation of Berg behind closed doors.

Berg would also find reasons, many of which bordered on infantile, ridiculous, or bizarre to go over and try to engage Klein in meaningless conversations. I suppose the reasoning for him was

 ©2015

that if he could get Klein to communicate with him, that things might go better. In Bergs world, communicating was defined as him talking endlessly at a rapid clip and the other person saying little or nothing, often standing in mortal fear as to what they were witnessing.

What Mitch Berg didn't realize is that these were really just opportunities for Klein to strike him down and humiliate him. Klein had made up his mind about Berg before I even started the job, and it was clear to me that once he made up his mind, that there was little chance of going back. Berg's rigid approach to Klein, and everything else, only reinforced this.

Berg knew he was getting pummeled at work, but had absolutely no idea how to de-escalate or find a way to change things between himself and Klein. He knew only one way, and that was to continue the entirely ineffective and abrasive things he was already doing.

In the meantime, Klein was seeking to line up behind him as many people as possible to join the anti-Berg bandwagon. Chief among them was Jim Azov, our co-worker. Another was a new hire he was about to bring on, Omar Ahmedy. He already knew that Mitch didn't approve of Omar, which

©2015

significantly increased the chances of Klein hiring him out of spite.

Jim was a smart and likable guy who knew how to do his job in sales very well. Klein had an almost erotic affection for him, as it seemed that in his bi-polar world, that as bad as Berg was in Klein's mind, Azov was every bit as good…..if not perfect. They were like two polar opposite twins in Klein's mind, his own version of Ying and Yang.

Azov,was no stranger to big company politics, and he sought to use this knowledge to his advantage as much as he could…and frankly, what choice did he have? It was either you were with Klein, who was the boss, or you were against him…that is to say, that you were with Berg. Klein made it very obvious that choosing sides was a requirement… and if you didn't, he would choose sides for you.

Azov wasn't one to wage such a negative campaign himself…but, he wasn't going to jeopardize his own position by opposing it either. This was counter to his nature, as Azov was the type of guy that rarely ever opposed anything people said directly…he was a master of affirming whoever was talking with him, even if he didn't necessarily agree with it. It's also what made him a good salesman, because people tend to agree with people that agree with them....and walk away liking them without even necessarily knowing why.

It wasn't to say Jim didn't know what was right or have backbone, but it was possibly more accurate to say he picked his battles very selectively most of the time.

Azov had been placed on a tightrope by Klein, and he handled it very well considering the circumstances. Because even though he knew Berg from a previous job like myself, he was also extremely annoyed by him. At the same time, I think he knew the campaign of irritation and harassment that Klein was waging was way over the line compared to pranks that may go on in a typical office.

At about 6p today, Berg was doing his usual end of the day cold calling on prospects. He always made it a point to stay longer than anyone in the department, despite the fact that his numbers were the lowest. In fact, he often stayed longer than anyone on the entire floor...which probably contained well over 200 people. However, Berg inhabited his own personal headspace that appeared stuck in some other time, as though logging hours in a sales job was what mattered, not closing actual sales. Remote offices,

©2015

smartphones and mobile email were something he didn't believe in, and certainly didn't use unless absolutely forced to do so against his will.

Anyway as Azov, Klein, myself and our newest hire Omar were walking out...Klein pulled out the power plug of Berg's computer while he was on the phone with a prospect. It was hard to imagine the VP of a department actively inhibiting sales in such a direct way, but we all saw him do it. Berg was immediately flustered, as most people would be. However, Berg was normally a very anxious person, and the constant fighting with Klein had only made him more so.

As soon as the call ended, Berg jumped out of his seat like some type of rabid maniac and ran directly up to Klein, chest to chest. Before I could even process what was happening, Berg began chest bumping Klein continually and in rapid succession. This had the effect of backing Klein up around the periphery of the floor as Berg continued to bump him over and over again, each time Klein stumbling backwards as Berg pursued him. These were two grown men...in some type of strange locker room harassment scene being played out 24 stories above New York City's financial district.

     ©2015

It went on for so long that I thought Berg might actually back Klein into a window and push him through it. The whole scene lasted for probably 2 minutes, which seemed like a very long time to be belly bucking your boss around an entire floor of an office building. I laughed in astonishment internally as I realized that Berg even managed to fight and show aggression in the most awkward way imaginable. It had a train wreck quality...you wanted to look away from the sheer embarrassment, but it was very hard to do.

Finally, the scene ended and Berg and Klein began talking heatedly. Even Klein, ever the instigator and troublemaker for all things Berg, realized he needed to calm the situation down quickly. Meanwhile, Omar and I quietly backed away and left for the elevators, eager to distance ourselves as quickly as possible.

As we went through the turnstile onto the street, Omar and I looked at each other with amazement and shock. He was about ten years younger than I, and had never seen anything like it. I had certainly seen guys yelling, swearing, throwing things and even pull down cubicles in anger...but I had never seen a subordinate belly thump his boss after his

©2015

boss deliberately unplugged his computer in the middle of a sales call.

It would all make a little more sense if we were working at a startup or some type of small shop run by an owner/operator. But we were weren't. Sharetech was a publicly traded global company with 15,000 employees. I was thankful that it took place at the end of the day when few people were around to witness it.

"Dude, that was some of most fucked up shit I have ever seen" Omar said.

"Yeah, really strange, juvenile and hard to watch." I replied

"Dude, that was like...embarrassing. Like what the hell is Klein doing unplugging his computer, and what is Mitch doing going off like some kind of little kid?....those two are seriously messed up. I can't believe this place...what is going on?" Omar seemed genuinely bewildered and shocked. I was less so, but it was still more than a little unsettling.

"Yeah...I hear you. That was extremely uncomfortable to watch."

©2015

We turned the corner on Water street and made our way toward the World Trade Center PATH station.

"Have you ever fuckin seen anything like that? What kind of a company is this?" While I understood what Omar was saying, he did seem to be almost enjoying his outrage at this turn of events. He continued.

"You know dude, I wasn't real sure about this job when I took it and the more time I spend here the more I think the whole thing is just bullshit. You got this Mitch guy acting like he is some type of manager and Klein who is out to get him... meanwhile, we aren't ever going to get paid on any of these sales we are making because it takes so much time for the revenue to come in. In the meantime, our salaries totally are lowball and we have to sit here while these two guys are going nuts everyday. I mean what the fuck am I supposed to think of that? That guy Mitch is no manager...he is a fucking joke!"

Omar definitely seemed to be taking it hard... probably a little too hard from my perspective, but I didn't argue with him....I just listened and agreed at the appropriate moments. It had been a

74   ©2015

very strange day, and we parted ways and walked to our separate trains.

Day 98 - Today we finished working on a big case, and Klein decided it was time for some celebrating with the team. However, this being Klein, he wasn't going to be straightforward about it...there had to be some subterfuge, some pain involved. I got an email from him around 1p.

"We are going out tonight to celebrate the end of the case and the good job you guys did...drinks are on on me. However, do NOT tell Berg.

Steve"

Of course Berg had worked the case just like the rest of us, but Klein apparently needed to keep ostracizing him as much as possible. I walked over to Steve and to see if I could get that reversed, not so much cause I wanted Berg to attend, but I knew it would be hard to lie about it in the days afterward. I really did not want to be involved with that distraction at all.

"Steve, I realize you don't like Berg, but you got to invite him, it's a team thing." I said.

 ©2015

"I am not fucking inviting that weasel...I can't stand to be with him and <Berg imitation> 'Heeey guys...' and his ' What type of whiskey do you have...is that an 8yr or 12 year single or blended malt'. He is fucking asshole and I don't want to have him along."

I laughed weakly at the Berg imitation, because it was spot on, and still continued trying to get him to take a different course of action.

"Steve, I get it, but you as the VP of our division have to realize that if he wanted to, Berg could make an HR issue out of this."

Klein was ostensibly an attorney, which was part of the reason that he got the job leading a team of legal sales people, but this fact was usually disregarded as his desire for pain and torture of Berg seemed to override any common sense for the finer points of the legal exposure he was placing himself and the company in.

"I don't really give a fuck about him, plus he's not going to find out if you guys don't say anything. And I know you guys won't say anything because you love your boss so much right?" Klein said.

I smiled weakly and said nothing. After being out of work for more than two years, I definitely

76

©2015

wasn't going to let my honor or righteousness get in the way of my kids having three regular meals each day, but it wasn't a particularly good feeling. Regardless, Klein had made it very clear that Berg was not going to get invited. He continued...

"Listen, once it gets later, we need to stagger our leaving times so he doesn't see us all walk out together. You know he will fucking stay until we are all gone, so we should pick a place to meet and then walk out at different times."

The decision was made to meet at a local bar a few blocks from the office. Once we all convened at the bar, Klein began an unrelenting bash session on Berg, complete with imitations of his voice and mannerisms. Omar immediately chimed in with his own admittedly spot-on imitation that veered into the ridiculous.

Klein had basically created a situation as the boss where his employees thought that to get on his good side, you needed to make fun of Berg and harass him. You were either with him or against him on this. I had tried to walk a middle ground, never one to join anyone's club regardless of the type, and certainly not this one.

          ©2015

However, Berg had made it difficult to stay impartial, because I had caught him trying to steal leads of mine that I would've freely given him had he asked. But he didn't...and then he lied about it when I asked him. It was completely petty and pointless, but thats exactly what he did. In doing so, he unwittingly played right into Klein's hand, and now I wasn't feeling too great about Berg either.

I had learned things about him over the years, and certainly on this job, that taught me he was always a guy who was very paranoid and concerned only about himself, which made his own self-destructive impulses even more baffling.

Truth be told, I wasn't a fan of either Klein or Berg, but I had to walk a thin line and try to stay as neutral as possible. Getting in pointless fights was not my purpose here, but suddenly it seemed as though it had become a job requirement. I considered every day, every month I was here a small victory....every paycheck another step away from the brink. I made sure my family got all of the healthcare appointments as up to date as quickly as possible in case I was suddenly out of work and lost my health insurance.

©2015

In fact, business wise we were doing well, in spite of the fact Klein was our boss and found little relevance in business matters that didn't directly relate to the continued harassment of Berg. Klein personally had a lot of money in his family and that made the explanation for this behavior slightly more understandable. In essence, it seemed he didn't feel he needed this job that badly and this helped him rationalize the indulgence of his darker instincts.

However, it appeared that each day he was sliding a little further over the edge with his behavior, as though Berg's overreaction and "belly bucking" incident let him know that you might be able to push him into oblivion. Lately, I sensed that Klein had decided that he may be able to get Berg fired without losing his own job. Whether this calculus was correct was anyone's guess.....

At the bar Klein really didn't have much to say after he was done bashing Berg....in fact, all roads seemed to lead back to this line of discussion...and whenever Omar did his over the top impression of Berg....Klein was always sure to laugh as hard as possible, with Azov and myself following close behind.

©2015

Leaving the bar later, I joked with Azov off to the side.

"Thank God that our primary mission is to hate Berg, as opposed to actually bringing in revenue. Anything else is secondary.....'How was work today honey?' 'Man, another great day of hating Berg...it was awesome!'". I said in mock triumph.

Azov started laughing hilariously, recognizing the insanity of the situation as I did, but not necessarily willing to go as far with openly expressing it within earshot of Klein. However, I was the top producer in the department for that moment, so I felt that I had more than a little leeway as long as I used humor instead of outrage or disdain. Or maybe I was just buzzed. I never directly criticized Klein....only tried to illustrate how crazy and pointless it was in a general way and perhaps hoping against hope this would help bring it to an end.

Klein laughed a bit when I did this, primarily because Azov did and he never wanted to be on the outside of Azov. If there could be a "bromance" between two co-workers, Klein was working hard to make it real, even though it was a one way street.

  ©2015

As the night wore on and the drinks took effect, the locker room mentality only intensified. Berg was a very intense cold caller, whose only real moments of solace seemed to come when he was on the phone pontificating in what seemed like very one sided sales "conversations".

The reality was, he was incredibly inefficient for the amount of time that he spent on the phone, but he did have passable numbers because he made so many calls. He also was almost pathological about following up very quickly with almost anyone who gave him a few precious moments of attention and that he may have sent information to. Often this resulted in him killing any chance he had with those leads, but the sheer law of averages meant he got some agreements back.

Meanwhile, Klein, as the manager, had the ability to listen in on his phone calls, which he did for what seemed like hours at a time. Apparently, the futility of Berg and the fact that people often hung up on him was a source of endless entertainment and fascination for Klein. Bergs' misplaced relentlessness also applied to the fact that he would often call leads on his cell phone so that the recipients caller ID would not identify him

    ©2015

as a solicitor. I suppose he hoped that he could grab a hold of a good sale once the prospect got over the fact Berg was deceiving them from the start. Interesting logic to say the least.

Likewise, any call that came in that he missed, even if it was overnight, he would call back as soon as he returned to his desk, just on the off chance that it may be a returned sales call, which it almost never was.

However, Klein saw an opportunity for further torture here, and an idea germinated while he was consuming his third beer.

"What we should do is call Berg and tell him that we are a big client and want to do business with him. Of course I can't do that, because he knows my voice, but one of you should do it."

By this time, Omar had been sitting near Berg for many months, and was firmly in the camp of hating him that Klein was in, mainly because he had to listen to his horribly annoying repetitive cold call schtick every day. However, he didn't have the intensity of maliciousness that Klein seemed to, more of an overall frustration we all had from just having to deal with his voice, and his personality, on the phone day in and day out.

©2015

He also, like Klein, did one helluva funny Berg imitation.

"Dude, I'll do it in a heartbeat..it will drive Berg nuts. All you really have to do is call him and block the number on your cell phone and he will go crazy trying to figure out who did it." Omar said

Thus, we were all reduced to enacting a 6th grade crank calling scheme at the behest of our boss, who really thought this whole idea was grand. The fact that it was something even his 13 year old son probably wouldn't do any longer seemed to totally escape him. If there was a way to torture Berg, it was always fair game in Klein's mind.

Meanwhile Azov, Ahmedy, myself and Klein laughed at the prospect of Berg, who was no doubt still sitting in the office at 6:30p, receiving a call from one of us, hoping beyond hope that someone was calling him back.

Still, it was one thing to laugh at the thought of it, it was another to actually do it. It was this point that Klein kept driving home until Ahmedy jumped on it. Omar had listened to too many of Berg's saccharin and phony sounding calls, and jumped on the opportunity to get what he probably

 ©2015

considered to be "payback". Klein goaded him on, reveling in the moment.

"He won't fuckin know who it is if you block the number. Just call him and hang up." Klein said

"Alright fine I'm going to do it...this is gonna be hilarious." Omar said.

Omar put the phone on speaker and dialed the office number and held the phone up on mute so we all could hear Berg's high pitched nasal voice answer. Everyone erupted in laughter as Omar hung up the phone.

After a few more times of this, it was enough to really get the grade school creative juices flowing as plans were concocted by Klein and Ahmedy of gradually increasing inanity. By the time they had finished, the idea was to impersonate a real client calling in and asking for his services. Azov volunteered that he would have a buddy who would be perfect. My silence or laughing was probably interpreted as approval, or more likely wasn't noticed at all in the fervor of alcohol fueled plotting.

After a few more crank calls, Klein grew restless and suggested we go to another one of his old haunts in lower Manhattan. According to him it

    ©2015

was a place he used to go when he worked downtown close to 20 years ago. Being the boss, nobody really was going to object.

"Now if I can just remember where this place is, I think it is still there. You guys are gonna love it. We used to go here for parties and sometimes after work." Klein said.

Because lower Manhattan is a confusing warren of old, narrow streets that often criss cross, we had some trouble finding it. This, in addition to the fact that it was dark and getting later meant the walk became long. Finally, a crappy storefront type place with a shitty neon beer sign came into view. A nagging feeling that Klein had totally oversold the place was creeping in. Basically, it seemed that whenever he said something was really good, you could be sure it was going to suck and he would get off on having misled you.

We then walked into what was a major-league hell hole of a bar. It was early in the week, and the few patrons that were there didn't look well. However the real kicker were the employees.

Klein had taken us to a low-rent strip/bikini bar that had some hideous looking people that shouldn't ever wear bikinis to go swimming, let

          ©2015

alone tend bar. These ladies were literally 100 pounds or more overweight.

"She is hot right Chris?" Of course, this was all part of Kleins fucked up bizarre paradise. Watching us squirm while he observed our reaction. Twisted was probably a too light a word.

"She is totally gross...really? You really used to come here and pay good money to sit in this place?" I muttered.

Jim and Omar looked at me like I had made a faux pas, but I didn't care. I had had a few beers and this was really just gross and strange. Holding back was never a skill that came easily to me, especially after several drinks.

"Chris what are you talking about, these girls are totally hot! Jim, this fucking guy doesn't know hot girls when he sees them" Klein said.

"I don't think so Steve...they are pretty hideous." I was happy to see Azov speak some truth to power. Though power was a flexible term in this case.

"When did you used to come here?" I asked

©2015

"Back in the early nineties, though I do feel that they were a little different looking back then." Klein said weakly.

Apparently Klein saw he was getting no support in his endeavor to promote the fantasy that this place was anything other than a horrific dive bar for people at the end of their rope. I tried to take advantage of the bad surroundings by getting a cheap beer and waiting until it was over.

Soon, we decided to leave once again, and I was thankful that that experience had ended as we ambled back down toward the South Street seaport. I then checked my watch, and realized I needed to hustle to catch the last train home. I made a hasty good bye and ran off into the night toward the World Trade Center PATH train as a light mist slowly settled down from above. I ran quickly, dodging the steam rising from Canal street, hinting at the pressure and heat just below the surface.

Day 100- Klein decides to have meetings several times a week with the "team" and today was no different. The point of these meetings is usually quite hard to figure out. Of course, the title of the

 ©2015

meeting always makes sense...but the actual content of what's discussed often steers into some sort of twisted digression that wanders off into the twilight zone.

Today was no different. We received an Outlook appointment for a 2p "team meeting."

As we walked into the meeting room at the appointed time, Klein began holding court.

"So...I've called everyone here to discuss whats going on with the cases and other things...blah blah blah....... I know that some of you have been doing well and signing some bigger deals, while OTHER people have been just bringing in agreements to bring them in and get their 25 dollar per-agreement bonus."

Klein continued, slowly building his negative momentum.

"I can tell you right now, I hate that.... and Andrew hates that as well. Believe me when I tell you, that the company is watching very closely, and they have NO problem shutting us down if people are just signing agreements to get their 25 dollar per agreement bonus and there is no revenue when it comes time to pay out later."

   ©2015

This bit of anonymous speaking was directed primarily at Berg, who was always concerned with his monthly per-agreement bonus more than anyone should be. Even if this didn't net him a big pay day down the road...his attitude seemed to be that he should get his 25 dollars now and not worry about later. I think the subtext of it was that he assumed he wouldn't be around when the deals paid out because he rarely lasted at a job more than 2 years anyway. Klein of course knew this, and also had the added benefit of being the one who constantly listened to his phone calls via the managers monitoring phone. Klein knew he was desperately signing smaller deals to "stuff" his numbers.

Needless to say, Berg immediately took the bait.

"It's not that we are signing agreements to just sign agreements. The fact of the matter is nobody really knows how much each agreement is worth until we get it in. Either way it can't hurt. What's the harm in it?" Berg said.

"The harm in it is that Andrew sees these agreements you bring in and knows that Joe's hamburger shack with a single location isn't going to bring in enough revenue for the company. He is sick of paying agreement bonuses for deals that

 ©2015

don't bring anything in." Klein replied, clearly annoyed.

Berg began turning red, as he did not ever have it in him to keep his mouth shut. He was going to defend himself, no matter what the cost. Meanwhile, Jim, Omar and myself all looked at each other across the conference table, knowing what was coming next and having trouble stifling a smile.

Berg continued with an aerosol spray of words.

"We all do the same thing and some of these accounts are big and some aren't, there really is no way to tell just by looking at the company. It's the law of averages. I've had instances where a small company had a very large claim, and a large company had a very small claim. It just depends on the industry, the company, and the type of claim we are working on." Berg stated forcefully in his nasal tone, his pitch rising with his intensity.

Klein continued...sensing blood in the water. His plan to draw Berg into a battle he couldn't win was working. The idea here was to get Berg to snap at him so he could refer the incident to HR and hurt his personnel file that way. Klein of course was too blind to see that this also would

©2015

eventually reflect badly on him as manager. He was too busy torturing his prey.

"Mitch, you were the first person I hired when they brought me in to start the department. I challenge you to name one small account that you have brought in that netted a large recovery with big revenue for the department."

Berg sat in his chair and shifted uncomfortably. His face was bright red, neck veins pulsing, because it never took much to get him angry, and this was doubly true when it came to Klein, who had evolved into his tormentor-in-chief. Klein took a perverse pleasure in his suffering. The fact that it was so easy to bring about only made it more pleasurable for him.

"What about Lodgview...that was a big account for the LCD settlement!!" Berg offered, apparently having what he thought was 'Eureka' moment.

It was true that Lodgeview was a decent sized company.

"First of all Lodgeview is a big company, but it didn't qualify for LCD..."

Berg blurted out. "Yes they did, they submitted a schedule of purchases and that should be a big

  ©2015

recovery for them and for the department." Berg felt he was on solid ground for but a brief second.

"Have you actually looked at what Lodgview does?" Before Klein could say anything else...Berg rushed to reply.

"Yes...they provide TV services for the lodging industry. They were happy to sign and I have an excellent rapport with them!"

"Yes...that's true. Do you know what the settlement is about? It's about overpriced LCD TV's and Computer monitors...the more screens or TV's a company purchased, the larger their potential refund."

Berg interjected again "Yes, I know that." he said, sounding very smarty pants about it.

"Fine, so I'll ask you again...do you even know what Lodgeview does? The provide in-room SERVICES for TV's in the lodging industry, not the actual TV's. That claim is essentially worthless or is very small...plus Andrew doesn't like the fact you signed them because they also handle porn services and he thinks that is a risk for the company. IF you would've bothered to look at what they do or bothered to ask a question maybe you would've realized that."

  ©2015

This last bit about Andrew, who was Steve's boss, was most likely completely fabricated, as was most of the rest of the supposed "angst" by upper management. In reality, they probably didn't know or understand what Klein was talking about. However, Klein wasn't going to miss a good opportunity to add fuel to the fire and mess with Berg's fragile egg-shell mind.

"It still could be a good claim, we haven't gotten anything back about it yet. You never know…. it can't hurt….. and I am more than happy to have a conference call with you and Andrew about that particular account if he wants to discuss it."

Klein continued, pouring more gasoline on the fire…

"I can tell you right now he doesn't want to have a conference call about it. I want you to understand the settlements and the class of companies that qualify for them and then sign bigger accounts and stop trying to take advantage just so you can get your 25 dollar monthly agreement bonus. That is not it's intended purpose and Andrew might take it away if he feels people are taking advantage of it unfairly."

 ©2015

Berg was now very agitated, and ready to fight this to the death, despite the fact he had already lost. Meanwhile, the rest of us sat there waiting for it to be over.

"He can't take away the per agreement bonus because of that, I've brought in more agreements here than anybody." Berg pleaded in a tone that was at once wounded and defiant.

"Actually that's not true...and you should have more total agreements because you've been here 8 months longer than the next closest person. On a per rep basis each month, your totals are among the lowest, not the highest" Klein fired back.

Now Berg was scrambling. I'd seen him like this before. He knew he was wrong, but it was not in his nature to admit that or ever back down. The facts had nothing to do with it because now his willful pride and sizable ego was on the line and he would charge into the hail of oncoming bullets no matter what.

"Er..well.... that's not true.... there were many months that I had more agreements than anyone, especially on the air cargo settlement and processed eggs."

    ©2015

Klein smelled blood. He was ready to spring his trap.

"Mitch, you know you did well on the Egg settlement because I gave you a list of qualified leads. All you had to do was call them. I stole that list from the last place I worked at. That's how I knew that they were qualified. Its not like you did some great job digging those companies up or finding them yourself."

"I still had to call and close them, which was more than had been done before I got here!" Berg spat out proudly.

"That's because you were the first hire, Mitch. There was nobody calling them prior to you getting here!" Klein said.

"That's not true...you tried to call a few and so did the call center."

Myself, Jim and Omar all looked at each with furtive glances around the table while Berg looked like a caged animal who was sitting up straight in his chair leaning forward with ferocious intensity whenever he spoke. The veins in his neck stuck out and he was red as a beet.

     ©2015

Outside, the helicopters filled with tourists and executives drifted by our window, oblivious to what was going on inside our little torture chamber of a conference room.

"Berg, I am not going to sit here and argue with you about this. You know exactly what I'm talking about...." Klein said.

"No I don't. I disagree with everything you are saying completely." Berg cut him off and jumped at what he apparently thought was his chance.

"Don't cut me off Mitch, the insubordination needs to stop right now"

It was always humorous when Klein brought up respect and the issue of insubordination in front of us, because this was coming from a guy who disconnected his own sales persons computer while he was on the phone trying to sell. However, he had shown a nearly equal capacity as Berg to deny the facts of the world around him and pick and choose what he saw as useful to whatever insane point he happened to think he was making at that moment.

Finally, Jim blurted out.

    ©2015

"Do you guys mind if we go back to our desks? Is the meeting over?" He apparently couldn't take any more of the grandstanding by the both of them. Klein interpreted this as another opportunity.

"See Mitch....See what you made me do? Now nobody can sit through a meeting with you because you make everyone so uncomfortable."

"I think that is you Steve, not me. " Berg always got the last word, no matter how bitter or asinine it was. Leaving well enough alone was not something he could ever do.

A very awkward silence persisted in the room for the next 20 seconds or so. Omar let out a laugh underneath his breath as the tension seeped through him along with the rest of us.

"Yes go ahead everybody." Klein said in his deadpan voice.

Later, I got an email from Klein. He had no problem sending all types of crazy emails through the company system. Inappropriate was not a word in his vocabulary.

"Chris, you do realize that that entire meeting was BS? Come see me." Klein's email said.

 ©2015

I ambled over to his desk, and he got up as we walked into small conference room. With the door shut he began talking.

"You do realize that entire meeting was BS right? Nobody has said anything about the agreement bonuses. That was all for Bergs sake because he is such a fuckin greedy weasel."

I was both relieved and astonished.

"So basically that was a fake team meeting designed to piss Berg off?"

"Correct."

"Wow. This is a new one for me."

"And just for the record, you are doing a great job and nobody has a problem with you, so don't get all freaked out. I could tell you were getting upset in there." Klein said.

He made it sound, at least to him, like that was an unusual reaction, as if everyone in the business world conducted fake meetings designed to demoralize and harass a single employee by disseminating false and misleading information to the whole team. How I was supposed to know this, I don't really know. However, I soon found out.

   ©2015

"I thought Jim already told you." Klein said.

Apparently he had shared his "fake meeting" plans with Azov, who wasn't sure if he was supposed to share it with me or not. Azov was part of Klein's "inner circle"....a circle that consisted of two people apparently. He had joked that I might be able to earn my way into this "inner circle" if I played my cards right. He treated this as sort of a joke that was really more serious in his mind than he let on.

"No, he never told me. I thought everything you said in there was real. Next time please let me know ahead of time. Why are we having fake meetings anyway?" I said.

"I told you why..... to mess with Mitch! Do you have a problem with that Chris?" Klein asked.

"I just think it's a waste of time. It seems to me that Berg has enough trouble without having those meetings. And quite honestly, if you want to fire him, my guess is that he has enough in his HR file to make that a reality also."

There was a long look that Klein gave me after this, as if to say "you just don't get it," It was almost as if being straightforward was not only an alien concept to him...it was something he had no understanding of. Backhanded double dealing, misinformation or strategic omissions were what he believed in...and he didn't seem to believe in these things for any career reason. It was more because he enjoyed messing with people purely for sport. In fact, I don't think his career concerned him, it was the fun of toying with his subordinates that gave him satisfaction, if it could be called that.

I envisioned a long line of previous targets of Klein's ire stretching back many years or even decades. Perhaps there was always a target like Berg, and always a minion who would enable the conduct like myself or Azov. Or perhaps not. Either way, it seemed like a well practiced skein of deceit that he weaved with frightening ease.

"Do you have a dungeon in your basement?" I blurted this out, apparently it had made it past the censor in my head.

However, the truth was, I was not as careful as I had been in previous months because I knew my numbers were good and he needed me. I also was just sick of the nonsense.

"What do you mean?" he said.

©2015

I smiled to him, signaling I was joking, but he knew the point I was making. An Ivy League graduate, Klein may be some type of sadist, but he wasn't stupid.

"I mean you seem like the type of guy who has a secret dungeon in suburbia and you torture people down there just for the fun of it, then put on your khakis and head out to the club like nothing happened." I stated flatly.

There was a good ten seconds of pause as I saw a flash of anger in his eyes. He knew I saw right through him...and I wasn't going to give him a free pass like Ahmedy and Azov did. I was older and had seen too much...plus I knew I had some power in the relationship due to my sales figures. I understood the business power game very well, having suffered under its rules for decades by now.

At the end of the day, Klein offered little in the way of value to the company, and he knew that. In a surprising bit of honesty, he was always the first to admit that "he was no salesmen"....a statement that could easily be the understatement of the year.

"Get out of here Chris.....that'll be the last time I fill you in on whats going on." Klein said,

    ©2015

seemingly frustrated at having been temporarily stopped in his tracks.

"Cmon Steve, you know I'm only joking.........sort of" I laughed after this...completing my mixed message to him. A little of his own fucked up medicine for good measure.

"Yeah right..." Klein said, his voice trailing off.

I could tell he didn't like what I was saying, because I had the audacity to call into question his behavior, and in his estimation, that wasn't allowed cause he was the boss. In his mind, being the boss was a license to do whatever he saw fit for those the reported to him. A blank check.

Day 124- The days seemed to have settled into a routine. The abuse and harassment of Berg, along with his completely inappropriate responses to it, seemed to have been normalized. It was as though this was who we were as a department, this was our culture.

I had joked with Azov before that our main goal as a department was hating Berg, that this had been a stated objective our manager, Steve Klein had communicated to us....and oh yeah..if you brought

©2015

in some sales that was OK too. But each day brought new emails to myself, Azov and Ahmedy about more fake meetings held for the benefit of "destroying" Berg, of fake phone calls made to his cell phone by outsiders set up by either Klein or Azov, designed to tell Berg he had missed out on a big sale.

Essentially, a three ring circus led by Klein to harass Mitch Berg day in and day out.

Rather than recognize this and fight back in a way that wouldn't show Steve Klein how mad he was or how vulnerable he was, Berg was unable to ever keep his cool when being baited by Klein....and this continually fanned the flames.

Mitch, much like Steve, also had a curious combination of being a sort of lonely lost puppy combined with a raging egomaniac who thought he was smarter than everyone else. He never failed to mention his own Ivy League degree or his perceived expertise as an intellectual Manhattan foodie that attended high-end whiskey tastings and managed to get to the best restaurants in the city, despite his constant cries of being poor-mouth.

 ©2015

He also loved to mention that he was "getting traction" with upper management, as if this would save him from the fact his sales numbers were mediocre. His idea of getting traction usually meant that if he saw someone in management in the hallway or the bathroom and they said "hello" to him and didn't ignore his presence, he was on his way to having an "in" with management, because everything was an imaginary angle that he was constantly working, usually to his own detriment.

Of course, Klein watched this with a combination of enragement and adolescent glee because it afforded him a wealth of opportunities to harass and drive Berg crazy.

One day, while Berg was at his customary 11:30a lunch, Klein called a snap meeting of myself, Ahmedy and Azov.

"Ok, here is the deal, I want everyone to wear suits tomorrow. But you CANNOT tell Berg." Klein said.

We all looked around, dumbfounded and smiling. We knew what this was, we just weren't quite sure how it would play out or what Klein had planned.

©2015

"Why do we have to do that? To mess with Berg!" Klein exclaimed, as laughter ensued.

"He will go nuts and think he is missing out on something if we all walk in in suits tomorrow. He will probably think we are having a meeting with management and that he is missing out on his big opportunity to get some 'traction'" Klein continued.

Truthfully, I think the idea had come from me as I had worn a suit a few days the previous week and saw how it generated such a fierce reaction. I jokingly mentioned this to Klein and well......here we were.

While all three of us laughed, we also kind of shook our heads at how stupid it seemed. However, nobody was going to bother telling the boss "no" on this one, as it was a simple enough request to fulfill.

Day 125- I woke early this morning and put on my suit as instructed. Quietly I was thinking to myself how crazy this whole thing seemed, and at the same time, was taking a quiet pleasure in knowing Berg would have a conniption trying to figure out what was going on. The fact that merely wearing a

 ©2015

suit might send him into a frenzy was sort of satisfying, if only because his overall demeanor towards everyone was relentlessly saccharin, selfish and phony.

I felt guilty for feeling this way, but at the same time, Berg did nothing but make matters worse for himself.

Because Berg was habitually late..or as he insisted, he worked later so he came in later, it made setting up the scenario that much easier. We were all in our seats wearing suits when he came in. He walked right up to my desk first thing, without even stopping at his own desk first.

"Is there a meeting today?" He was already very amped up and nervous. His eyes looked scared and his face was already red. It was barely 10a, but he looked like he had seen a ghost.

"Not that I am aware of….." Before my voice even ended, Berg cut me off.

"Then why did you wear a suit?!?" His tone was as abrasive as a cop asking for your ID at a teenage party.

"Because I wanted to…" I said.

106   ©2015

Berg said nothing and immediately s stormed away from my cubicle and marched right over to Kleins desk. I couldn't hear everything that was coming out of there, but the tone on both sides was confrontational and aggressive and followed the usual pattern of Berg pushing relentlessly for answers while Klein skillfully gave little away. As an attorney, he was a master of the non-answer answer...and this served to drive Berg further into temporary madness.

Before long...Berg was shaking and beginning to cry. A grown man crying standing next to his bosses cubicle because he couldn't get an answer as to why people were wearing suits. Not blubbering, but beat red and rubbing his eyes, voice quaking.

"So is there a meeting today?" Berg said shakily.

"No Mitch, there is no meeting..." Klein reassured him.

Before Steve could finish his sentence, Mitch broke in again, voice intense and direct.

"Then why is everybody wearing suits? Why would everybody be dressed up if there wasn't some type of meeting that you didn't tell me about?"

    ©2015

Normally, Klein would've have used this opening to concoct some type of story or lie that would further exacerbate the situation, but even he was momentarily stopped by the ferocity of Berg's intensity and volatility.

"There is no meeting....they just decided to wear suits."

"Why? Why didn't anyone tell me??" Berg said, somehow managing to sound both threatening and pathetic at the same time.

"I don't know. It's not a big deal. Why don't we go downstairs and talk about it..."

Klein realized that he had to back down or face having a full blown incident on his hands. He had underestimated how on edge Berg really was yet again, and sought to get him out of the office to try and decompress the situation with some fresh air.

Meanwhile Jim, Omar and myself huddled around Jim's cubicle, flabbergasted by what we had just seen.

"I think he was actually crying...unbelievable." I said.

  ©2015

"I don't think I've ever seen anything quite like that. He is totally on the verge of something bad. I wouldn't be surprised if he comes in here with an automatic weapon and goes off on all of us." Jim said

"He's a fuckin pussy...crying over that in front of everyone. That was completely crazy." Omar added

Jim was right. I don't think any of us really fathomed how close to the breaking point Berg was, and how much closer Klein had pushed him to it over the last several months. Clearly, the campaign of intimidation and harassment was having its desired effect for Klein. As usual, he was blind to the fact that it could easily take him down with it.

Klein was like a bomb maker who was very close to being taken out by his own explosive device.

Berg had reacted viciously right from the moment he got to work. Nobody had said a word to him, we only had walked in dressed up, and he immediately stomped over to Steve's desk to find out what was wrong and how he was being slighted. While this reaction was anticipated given his previous track record, it still was amazing to

109 ©2015

see how 'on cue' he responded to a fairly innocuous provocation.

Of course, without realizing it, Berg had brought much of this on himself. We all were tired of his delusional and incessant talking about how he was feathering his career nest with management, asking us what our monthly numbers were, and his obsessively watching of the monthly sales report so he could compare himself and ask us how many more deals we expected to get in.

The funny part of this last bit was that Berg was never the leader in sales numbers...but he watched it as though he was. He almost seemed to derive some perverse pleasure from his constant falling short. Misery was his constant companion, and Klein only sought to amplify this at every turn. I think Klein also recognized such a state of mind quite easily.

I think after what we later began calling the "suit day", we all, save for Klein, realized that Berg might be capable of things, if pushed far enough, that were a bit frightening.

Later in the day, Jim saw a story on CNN about a man in midtown Manhattan who had shot two of his co-workers right in the office at the Empire

©2015

State Building. He then fled down the elevators to street level where cops in the heavily guarded area began pursuing him. A gunfight had ensued right on West 33rd street that ended up hitting a bystander and ultimately killing the gunman himself. A cop was also injured.

As we read more about it, it concerned a small office in the garment industry where a longstanding feud had developed between a sales person and a designer. The salesperson was vocal and well liked, but also pushy and forceful.

The designer was more of an artistic type, who was quiet and had been in a series of circular, escalating feuds with the salesperson that had stretched back for many years. Apparently, one day, the designer had snapped after being laid off, and decided to come back to the office to exact revenge on the persons he deemed responsible for this, which included the salesperson.

An escalating longstanding feud....this sounded all too familiar to us, and after the 'suit day', we all had a clearer understanding of how such things could develop given the right mix of personalities, bad behavior, and circumstances. The three of us, Azov, Ahmedy and myself, looked at this story with more than passing curiosity.

 ©2015

To us, it was a cautionary tale, or perhaps a window into a possible future.

Day 135 - During the course of our work, the weather wasn't normally a big topic of discussion. However as the week had ground on, it had come to be a topic of growing chatter around the office. When CNN started blaring late Thursday into Friday about Hurricane Sandy possibly hitting New York with a "direct hit", we had to let down our hard boiled "seen it all" attitude and begin to consider what was happening.

The forecast seemed to call for deteriorating weather over the weekend, with the possible strike occurring on Tuesday of the following week. As with all such forecasts, there was a fair amount of uncertainty as to what exactly would happen, but the fact that our office was in the worst flood zone in lower Manhattan meant that if a direct hit did occur, we were probably going to be severely affected.

Steve didn't really address this at the end of the week, but he told myself and Azov he would be in touch if any new updates came about.

   ©2015

Recently, Klein had decided that Ahmedy was beginning to creep "outside" of his so-called "circle of trust" because he rarely came to work on time, often found excuses for long excursions away from the office during the day and most importantly, his production sucked and he didn't seem to care about it. He sort of gave the impression that he was just collecting the "corporate" salary, or at least that's what Klein thought, and Klein was very much about people either being in or out of his "circle".

Playing favorites wasn't a low key management tool of his, but an in-your-face exercise of divide and conquer. What exactly he was conquering was left up to one's imagination, but shunning people for real or perceived slights was his way of letting you know something was going wrong. I had also heard whispers of Ahmedy being called into meetings with Klein and HR over his performance reviews. If this was true, the animosity was probably growing between them.

Regardless, Klein let us know that Jim and myself were now the A-team, but that as two equal pigs in his Orwellian Animal Farm, Azov was more equal. For the most part this didn't faze me, as I was old enough to see Klein for what he was..an

    ©2015

impotent fool with an Ivy league degree who worked hard to prove his fictional stature in life. As long I got credit for my sales and got paid what was coming to me and our department survived, my attitude was that I could put up with most anything. Or at least that was what I needed to believe.

"I'll let either Jim or you know when I hear something from the facilities people about the hurricane. You'll also get company wide emails I would think, though you never know with this fucking place." Klein had said before we left for the weekend, getting in his last dig on our employer.

Klein not only hated half his employees, he made a regular habit of disparaging the company in general as "cheap" and "fucked up". Making enemies was a sort of national pastime for him, when he wasn't taking up his work days stalking our personal lives or various women on the internet or in the office, he was listening in on Berg's phone calls for hours on end to no real purpose. This was what passed for management in his estimation. Either that or he just flat out didn't care.

  ©2015

"I'll also have to go over to my parents this weekend and keep checking up on them because they will have watched CNN and gotten completely nervous about the weather." he said.

His parents, specifically his dad, were topics that were increasingly being discussed by Klein as they were still semi-independent, but well into their 90's. They lived near him and some of his other siblings out on Long Island. Whenever he could, he would let us know that his Dad had "built half of New York", but when pressed for specifics, the picture seemed to dissolve into a series of generalities and his "blah blah blah's" that he didn't seem to want to discuss.

"My mom drives my dad nuts with the CNN and Fox news watching and her worrying, and he has got some serious health issues so I will need to go over there and keep them calmed down." Klein said.

On some level, it was good to see that Steve had a shred of concern for somebody. At this point, the bar had been lowered so far in my mind that seeing him express concern for other people seemed shocking, even if it was his elderly parents who were facing a major hurricane for the first time in their lives.

     ©2015

Day 138- The weekend had passed, and the previously "uncertain" predictions were now turning into "almost certain" dire warnings. New York City was going to be hit by hurricane Sandy, it was just a matter of where and what time it would occur. The attitude at work was fairly calm. Our company was setup to handle these types of events due to our global nature as a financial services company, and there were procedures in place for an orderly close down.

Of course, Klein did not want to miss this golden opportunity to ratchet up Bergs anxiety level even higher. He started with his usual 'information lockdown' on Mitch. To Berg, this was true torture because the one thing he craved from people was interaction. He often didn't care if it was negative, he just liked the back and forth and the constant debating and bickering.

This, coupled with the fact he was fairly anxious to start with, meant that Berg was looking around over the top of his cubicle for evidence of the three of us meeting without him. On those occasions when he thought he saw such a meeting taking place, he would often walk right over and announce.

   ©2015

"So am I missing anything? What are you guys talking about?" Berg would say shamelessly.

This of course, made all of us not want to tell him anything, because the tone was at once both commanding, irritating and abrasive. The look on his face was always of utmost seriousness and concern.

"What's going on with the Hurricane... are we coming in tomorrow?" Berg said loudly.

By this time, everyone knew that forecasters were calling for a late Tuesday evening landfall. Today was Monday. Everyone....... except Berg, who often like to play like he was too busy to be bothered with such trivialities as weather. He also was a master of asking questions he already knew the answer to, just to gauge if Klein would lie to him.

"Well Mitch, its supposed to hit tomorrow, so I doubt that" Klein said.

"Oh really? I heard that it wasn't going to be that bad until later in the evening so I figured that we could get in early and make some calls before we pack it in in the afternoon."

It was these types of statements that were both annoying and baffling. Annoying because there was

 ©2015

always a thought behind them by Berg that was meant to push a major theme of his....namely, that he was worthy because he worked harder than anyone else and was always willing to "go the extra mile."

Never mind that this had little basis in reality. He was willing to make these ridiculous "stay late" statements at least once a week to just about anyone who even appeared to be listening. That often meant anyone who was standing within a five foot radius.

Usually, he was the last to leave and would always feel compelled to let us know that he was "staying late to make some California/West Coast calls". Whether this actually happened was a great source of speculation amongst all of us until one day Klein checked the call records and found it to rarely be true.

Essentially, he stayed late because he wanted to, and wanted to be seen by others as the last guy to leave the office. Apparently, the idea that this could advance his career came completely out of thin air, as the culture at Sharetech was not one where people were burning the midnight oil constantly to show their superiors how hard working they were. In fact, most of the people

©2015

that Berg thought he was impressing left the office before he did...but he took comfort in the fact that they saw him on the phone when they walked out.

Never mind the fact that by this point, Klein had made sure that Berg had been called into various HR meetings and probably had a very thick file of infractions and mediocre reviews to boot. His record was not exactly clean, and his performance as a salesperson, while not terrible, wasn't great, especially when considering the number of hours he spent there.

"Well Bloomberg says there are shutting down the subways at 5p tonight. I guess this is only the second time they have ever done that in New York City." Azov offered up.

"Well I'm sure if its not bad they will be back on tomorrow." Berg said, as if he had a burning need to believe this completely ridiculous false statement.

"Mitch, tomorrow is Tuesday, the day Sandy is supposed to strike. Its supposed to be here tomorrow evening. Opening and closing the subways is a big deal. It takes a lot of time." Ahmedy said to him, clearly annoyed with Berg.

 ©2015

"Oh, I hadn't read that. But I just thought that if we could be productive for a few hours that would be a good idea." Berg said.

The fact that he was rarely that productive was lost on him completely. The sheer denial in Berg's ongoing comments showed an almost pathological need to either be right, or deny reality. Part of everyone's frustration with him was rooted in the fact the Berg never missed a chance to tell anyone and everyone that he was a consummate New Yorker who "grew up in Bensonhurst Brooklyn", but somehow failed to grasp how big a deal shutting down the subways was. He seemed to indicate that he thought it was possible to turn them off and on like a light switch, and that would enable him to make it to work the following day…..simply because he thought that is how it should work, the facts be damned…and because he had a deep "need" to be at work, despite the fact it was a source of constant misery for him.

It was almost as though he had envisioned a fantasy scenario where he was in the office during the day of the hurricane as the only "intrepid" employee who bothered to show up.

He would don his headset and make his horrible cold calls in his best Willy Loman imitation, and

©2015

then just while he was pontificating loudly and the wind was howling outside, senior management would parade by his desk and quietly give him the "thumbs up" for being the one reliable guy who made it into Sharetech the day Sandy struck.

It was like something out of a Jimmy Stewart movie, but Berg, given his idiotic statements to us, almost seemed to think it could actually happen.

The reality was, Sharetech didn't want people coming to work that day because it represented a liability to the company as well as to the employees. A hurricane bearing down on New York was big news, and they didn't need to do anything to shine a negative spotlight on the fact that their offices were located in a highly vulnerable flood zone.

Needless to say, all of this sort of logic seemed lost on Berg, who was still insisting that coming in on the Tuesday of a once-a-century hurricane strike was a plausible idea.

Tonight, Azov and myself were texting regarding business and our ability to log into our email online. Berg, being a self professed "not good with computers person" had never bothered to figure

 ©2015

out how to login remotely from home. However, it was now becoming crucial that we did so, as it became fairly apparent that the worst case scenario was about to play out. We would be out of the office for at least two days or longer.

This meant that Azov had to get in touch with Berg and give him instructions on how to do this, as it was something Klein would never do, and Berg was requesting email access help very insistently. Needless to say it got complicated quickly, and Berg apparently turned it into a 45 minute back and forth conversation. According to Jim, the conversation ended with Berg stating once again that "he'll only log in remotely if he didn't go in tomorrow", despite the fact we had already been told by the company not to come in.

As for Omar, he had access to his needed email, but it was highly questionable whether he was actually concerned about it either way. Klein had told us to stay at home, but other than that, had not bothered to stay in contact with any timely updates about what was happening beyond what the company wide emails we received had already said.

©2015

All of us, and the rest of the New York City metro area, waited in the meantime for the storm to hit, unsure of exactly what to expect.

©2015

I didn't care what he said about me….I was way beyond that. My brother had gone off to summer camp, and my other siblings had gone to my grandparents house.

Somehow it became me, my mom and him….and the dogs. We were sitting at the dinner table, the candelabra blazing. The silver shined to perfection. The old man sat there with an ash tray next to his perfectly aligned place setting while he waited to be served his evening meal.

I took my place in the middle of the table, with my Dad at the head and my mother at the other end. Her spot was empty while she was in the kitchen, putting the finishing touches on dinner.

Outside, a ferocious snowstorm was picking up, making the wind howl and buzz inside the old metal storm windows. He just sat there, exhaling smoke and looking off into empty space. We sat for what seemed like forever in silence while I heard my mom's clanging in the kitchen. Not a word was said until he finally spoke between wind gusts.

"So..do you think you'll ever amount to anything?" I suppose he meant that toward me, but he wasn't looking...just staring off into space.

©2015

I hated these questions, because I knew that it was some sort of test where I would inevitably fall short of whatever expectation he had cooked up in his head. Being all of 12 years old, the right answer was hard to come by.

"Uhm, yeah I guess so" Silence. Another long inhale and then an exhale as the windows rattled and I watched the snow piling up outside the French doors on our back porch.

My mom, who hated smoking but was well practiced in stifling her frustration, walked in with a huge plate of pasta and set it down in front of him. He did not acknowledge her, but continued staring forward, as if watching a movie that hovered somewhere on the opposite wall.

For the next 5 minutes, he sat there, disregarding everyone and smoking in silence. I gave a furtive glance to my Mom, who finally asked him to pass the food if he wasn't going to have any.

He didn't move, prompting her to ask me to "Please pass the pasta"

Because the plate was so big, I was not able to hold it while sitting. I was going to have to get up and go get it, as my father made no move to do

 ©2015

anything. He seemed completely checked out, or in his own world.

As I slowly rose, fear began welling up within me. I heard only the sound of rapidly moving air outside, and remember glancing briefly at the few flakes emerging from the shadows that hit the light coming from our windows. I began taking a step toward my Dad, and watched as he slowly disconnected himself from his revelry and turned his head toward me. I took another step as I watched his eyes lock in on me, unsmiling in their darkness and disapproving at my very existence. The fear of his gaze was immediately within me, and I began to shake as I neared his seat.

"Did you want some Dad?" I muttered.

Silence, then he put his eyes down.

I reached out to grab the enormous circular bowl as the smoke curled up around the ashtray and toward the ceiling. Then, his hand reached out to grab my arm. He squeezed my elbow hard for a second, and then released it while he looked me straight in the eye.

"No." he said "I don't want anything from you."

 ©2015

*I slowly stepped backward toward my seat,
keeping my eyes on him as he glared, and then his
head turned, back to his inner space as the silence
crept back, slowly smothering the room.*

©2015

Day 139 – We were notified by intracompany email that we were not required to come in today given the situation with the Hurricane that was almost on top of the city. Jim and myself both had email access to the company from home, so we knew what was happening. We had also texted a few times.

I spent the day waking to some high clouds, which gradually thickened a bit by lunchtime. The kids came home from school early as most places had begun preparing for the worst.

However, none of us, as far as I could tell, heard anything from Steve, our erstwhile manager. Everything we heard regarding the storm was general company email, or us talking/texting amongst ourselves, which for most of the day consisted of myself and Azov. Ahmedy really didn't care what went on at work for the most part, and Berg didn't really text, as he considered that beyond his scope and he did not own a smartphone that made it easy.

By late afternoon, I had begun using masking tape to make large "X's" on the picture window in our living room as well as all the ground floor bedroom windows. They were projecting winds in excess of

 ©2015

100 miles an hour so I wanted to be as safe as possible.

In the early evening I had talked to Azov on the phone and he told me the Berg had spoken to him inquiring again how to check his work email. He also was apparently still talking about waiting for the subways to start running so he could maybe "get in and make a few calls." The fact that we had discussed 12 hours earlier that this was impossible did not seem to effect him one way or the other. As far as Berg was concerned, he had no apparent memory or acknowledgement of that conversation.

By 9pm that evening, I had put the kids in the basement along with my wife while I sat up in the bedroom tracking the internet and the coverage on TV, trying to figure out how bad this was going to get while also texting family back home in the Midwest. The winds had grown very strong, and with each gust on my second floor windows, I could feel the whole house shake. I thought a few times that the roof coming off was a real possibility as lights flickered with each mammoth gust of wind.

On my laptop screen, I watched the train station at Hoboken fill up with several feet of water while

 ©2015

the PATH train tube under the Hudson was now really just a 18 foot sewer pipe filled with storm surge. A huge transformer exploded near our office, and all of lower Manhattan went dark.

By late the next morning, images of destruction were everywhere on TV, as people without power huddled around jerry-rigged outlets in midtown that they had walked miles to reach. Staten Island had been hit very hard as had the Jersey Shore. Rumors had it that the entire 6 story subterranean parking garage of our building on Water street was filled with over 70 feet of water from storm surge. New Jersey Transit had images of boats and barges sitting on the tracks or pushed up over bridges. Most of the subway system was totally flooded, and salt water had corrupted most of the electrical gear.

It appeared we would not be reporting to work for a very long time.

Day 158 – After a few weeks of being at home, we got word that we were going to be transferred to another office of Sharetech that was located just across the Hudson river in Jersey City. While the NJ Transit trains were still not running, I was able to get into the city via bus and then take the PATH, partially restored, out to our new location.

©2015

Upon arrival after my very long commute, it was clear to me that these were offices that hadn't been occupied in any real way since the early 90's. We, along with perhaps 30 other various displaced people from our office were located on a floor that was designed to hold perhaps 600 people. Somebody joked it reminded them of a scene out of the Walking Dead TV show....but I saw no Zombies upon my entrance into the building.

When I arrived, Steve said to me "Where the fuck were you?"

"It took me two and a half hours to get in Steve, not much I could do about it." I offered.

If I were Berg, he probably would've gone off on me for the next 20 minutes. But because I wasn't, and despite his appetite for conflict, he instead decided to drop it. I'm sure that in his calculus, it was better not to alienate a good employee when your main target was elsewhere.

Klein was intensely focused on the new seating chart for our department in this space, and how he could effectively isolate Berg from the group without being caught. Meanwhile, I was focused on a big batch of new agreements I had managed to

©2015

bring in from a business trip, but Steve acted liked he couldn't be bothered to discuss that.

Klein had sent around an email that reminded me of a note a second grader would pass around to their friends. The email showed the seating "pecking order" for the department. His favorite, Jim Azov, was seated directly next to him. He then told me that I was sharing a wall with him and was directly opposite. Omar was next to Azov, and Berg had been placed in an entirely separate cubicle cluster several desktops away to drive home the point that he was unwanted. Meanwhile, our section of the floor was almost entirely empty. We also had a part time worker with us who was doing database work, and she was sitting directly opposite and behind me.

Klein told us this arrangement was temporary, and that he had been told by facilities that we were eventually going to be moved to a newer Sharetech building across the street. However, he did not know how long our stay would be. We also had a few other workers from other Sharetech departments down an open corridor from us, some of whom would be witnessing Klein's activities for the first time.

 ©2015

Day 161- Because our office was almost completely vacant, people felt, rightly or wrongly, that they could speak freely. There was no senior management, no room full of witnesses for bad behavior...no need to check your speech at all.

Both Berg and Klein took advantage of this situation. However, it was Mitch who slipped up first.

He was speaking with Felice, our database temp who also happened to be a woman of color and a college graduate of NYU who was pursuing her MBA. In the meantime, she was keeping some money coming in by working for us.

Mitch, who fancied himself something of a liberal intellectual, no matter how divorced from reality this was, decided to start talking politics with her.

Felice is probably one of the nicer, most non confrontational people I have worked with, so it was dumb luck that Berg picked her and not somebody else who may have reacted a little more violently.

Berg had been blathering on about the recently completed presidential election and he asked Felice whom she voted for, which can be a dangerous move in a work setting unless you are

 ©2015

very close with the person, which needless to say, Berg was not. However, that never had stopped him in the past.

"I voted for Obama, he really seemed better than Romney to me. But my grandmother doesn't like him and would not vote for him." Felice said.

"Yeah, but your grandma is black as well correct?" Berg blurted out

"Well yeah she is...."

Berg cut her off as only he could

"So why wouldn't she vote for Obama?" he spat out, unknowing how abrasive and ignorant he sounded.

"I don't know I guess because she didn't like him..." At this point, another woman who was working near us, spoke up because she was clearly peeved at how insensitive and intrusive Berg was being.

"Why would you say that Mitch? Why would you just assume that you know who her grandma voted for or who she would vote for? That's crazy!" she said.

   ©2015

At this point, Mitch turned bright red and began trying to backpedal, immediately realizing he had been caught showing his racist tendencies that didn't comply with his self-image as a liberal, open-minded New Yorker. who dutifully read the New York Times on a daily basis.

"I didn't mean that, it's just that I thought she would vote Obama because that seems like a natural choice. Listen, I'm a Jew, if Bloomberg were running for president I would've voted for him because he's Jewish, so I'm no different than anyone else."

Of course this kind of statement only served to highlight the idiotic assumptions he was making to begin with, rather than alleviate the tension.

What I was hearing as intense awkwardness, Klein was hearing as a distinct opportunity to get rid of Berg. At the very least, he could potentially use this information, if played properly, to hurt him very badly. Klein said nothing, but, as I would soon find out, he was taking everything in behind his cubicle wall.

 ©2015

Day 160- As I walked in this morning, I saw Azov standing by Kleins desk, which was often his morning post. Klein always got in early, and usually Jim was the next person in. Most mornings Klein would summon his favorite guy to his desk to listen to God knows what. Often the topics surrounded who he was stalking online, like ex-college girlfriends from 30 years ago, which celebrities or public figures had been caught in extremely compromising positions, and of course, what he had on tap for his daily dose of Mitch Berg harassment.

As I learned later, today was no different than any other day for Klein. He viewed the conversation he had heard Berg having with Felice a few days earlier as a sort of call to arms.

"He's fuckin done" he said to Azov and myself.

"Did you hear that shit? That was some of the most racist, unprofessional behavior I'd ever heard." Klein said.

While what Klein was saying wasn't untrue, the fact that he was passing judgment on anyone's workplace professionalism was laughable at best.

"Where does he get off harassing her like that?... anyway...I'm going to talk to Julie the admin who

©2015

heard the whole thing. I think this definitely needs to go to HR as he was harassing Felice with all that racist crap about Obama. It clearly also bothered other people around him...just ask Julie..... It bothered you too, right Chris? Could you believe what was coming out of his mouth?"

I had to pick my words carefully, because while I thought Berg did seem like a total ass, and perhaps a slightly bigoted one at that, I didn't think it was worth bringing down a big corporate HR scenario onto our department. My main reason for thinking this was twofold...the first being that, while it was annoying and unprofessional, the main person involved, Felice, wasn't really upset by it. The only person who was upset was the admin Julie, and she was upset on Felice's behalf because she could sense the inappropriateness of what Berg was saying.

"Yeah, well it was pretty lame, and certainly not politically correct, but I'm not sure we need start an HR case about it....seems like a bad move because that never ends well for anyone in the department." I stated

"What? You heard that crap Chris, he was totally out of line! Would you be willing to go into HR as a witness if necessary?" Klein said.

 ©2015

This was an easy one. Going to HR was like snitching to your parents or the police. In no way was it going to help my career, and probably wouldn't solve the problem of Berg and Klein either.

"Sorry Steve, can't do it. I also didn't really hear the whole thing because when it started getting weird I actually got up and walked away, so I'm not sure that I am such a good witness."

"Whaaat? Oh so now you are going to be a wimp about it? C'mon, you won't get in trouble because you didn't do anything. You would just be reporting on what you heard. I know Jim would do this for me if I asked him.... right Jim?"

Jim stood there, with his hands up, clearly not wanting to be in this position.

"Well, I'm not sure I'd go that far...." he said and then trailed off.

Steve assessed that his effort to rally the troops wasn't going quite as well as he thought it would.

"Fine I'll talk to Julie. She is the best person anyway because she heard the whole thing and was clearly upset by it."

   ©2015

Klein also seemed to think that because she was a woman and not in the executive or sales ranks that she might be more easily 'convinced', if not bullied, into going on the record with HR about the incident between Berg and Felice. He wasn't above pulling rank to get what he wanted when it came to Berg. In fact, he relished the opportunity to throw his weight around.

We heard later that day that Steve had made a call to HR to log the incident with them. It seemed to be lost on him that the constant meetings with HR that always involved both he and Berg only served to make both of them, and by association the department, look bad. I was amazed at the fact that Klein never seemed to realize this, despite the fact he clearly was intelligent. He seemed to have a hard time putting it all together because he was so blinded by his need to exact revenge and pain on Berg. It was the only thing he was able to stay focused on during the work day.

 ©2015

Day 162 – Each day as I come in, I am granted the privilege of sharing a wall with Klein under the new seating arrangement. Klein always comes in early, leaving his house sometime near 6a each day. Why he does this I'm not quite sure, but I'm starting to wonder if it is to conduct his phone conversations that I am forced to listen to each day. In the old office, my seat was further away and I was only vaguely aware of them. Now I had a front row seat.

These conversations often remind me of a high school freshman gossiping to friends for hours on end in the most bitter and caddy way. The main difference being that every conversation is littered with loudly spoken F-bombs in the middle of an office setting.

Klein was, as usual, oblivious to how bad he looked, and because there were very few people in these temporary offices, he felt more emboldened than usual. I surmised after listening to many of these talks that Klein was speaking to some attorney friend of his who also apparently had hours during the work day to discuss just about anything and everything that they could. However, it was always highly negative, bitchy, and often vaguely sexual. I also surmised that

140   ©2015

Klein had been, or was attempting to, cheat on his wife. He seemed to really like bragging about this sordid business. Who it was with, I couldn't easily make out...though I wasn't really sure if it was a man or a woman. Either way, I didn't really care.

Needless to say, it wasn't a lot of fun sitting here listening to this, and I found myself astounded that someone north of 50 years old would actually sit and do this for several hours each day, then hang up the phone and direct his ire at Berg, who, for all his annoying faults, at least attempted to work and bring in business in his own way.

Day 180 – During the morning "stand around Steve's desk and pretend to like him" session with myself and Azov, Klein mentioned to us that the HR meeting regarding Berg and his "racist" comments had occurred, and that he had indeed drawn Julie into the proceedings to go on record that these comments bothered her. While that may have been true, I'm sure she also felt pressured by Klein to go on record because he was an executive, and probably felt it was better for her career to go along with it rather than forget about it. Klein had managed to draw yet another person into his darkening web.

141   ©2015

Day 183 – We had gone on one of Steve's mandated afternoon coffee runs when he told myself and Jim that word had come down we would be switching offices yet again. This time we were moving across the street from the "Walking Dead" office where we currently were to a newer space. He told us that a meeting was to follow shortly, but not without letting us know that he was going to make it nice and painful for the benefit of Mitch Berg and his fraying nervous hold on reality.

Day 185- All of us got an email this morning from Klein informing us that we were going to have a meeting that afternoon. At 3p we found ourselves seated around a large conference table yet again. Klein seemed to always get a particular charge out of presenting the darkest and most negative aspects of whatever it was he was discussing

"As you know, we have been here at the offices of 525 Washington for the last few months since the storm came through. I know that many of you who live in the city are hoping to be able to move back to the 199 Water street location. However, I am here to tell you that that is not going to ever, ever

  ©2015

happen, so just forget about it. That office is gone for good, and Sharetech no longer is going to be renting that space because we were planning to leave anyway and the damage is too extensive. So get used to it...." Klein said, pausing as he let this information settle in.

This of course was ostensibly directed at everybody, but was really aimed at Berg, because he was the one who had obsessively been asking about returning to that office as it was much closer to his home on Roosevelt Island, and he viewed working in Manhattan as more prestigious. And the image of prestige was very very important to him.

Just like clockwork, he chimed in on cue.

"So that means we aren't going back to 199 in lower Manhattan" Berg said.

Klein spat out "Yes, that's what I just said Mitch, didn't you hear me?"

"Yeah, yeah right right, I just wanted to clarify...is there a possibility that I could work out of the office that we have in midtown rather than coming out to Jersey City every day? It's a lot more expensive for me...." Berg stated.

 ©2015

"No, there is no way that anybody in that office wants you there Berg" Klein shot back

"Well did you ask, because it seems to me that...." Of course Mitch was never going to stop, was not going to shut up.

"I didn't ask, because I know what the answer is Mitch. Let me tell you something...let me tell all of you something. This company hates us...we are nothing but a pain in the ass to them and the last thing that I am going to do is start asking for favors. As a matter of fact, when we move into our new offices over at 480 Washington, we are going to be around a bunch of people who hate us, and you had better realize that right now. Nobody wants to hear your little anecdotes, I don't want to see people going around looking for free food. These people have worked here a long time and have no interest in new people coming and sitting next to them making loud annoying phone calls all day. Upper management is keeping a close eye on what is going on.....you see this shitty office we are in now? The reason we are here is because nobody wants to be around us. So lets forget about asking for special favors."

©2015

One thing to say about Steve Klein, he knew to how bring a sales force to the edge of suicidal mania.

As I looked around the room, Jim, myself and Omar flashed brief looks and alternated rolling our eyes and shaking our heads. Needless to say Berg was beyond dejected. We knew Klein was nuts, but nobody likes to hear that the "whole company" they work for hates them, even if you know it isn't true. Klein continued talking about the housekeeping aspects of the move, and the dates of our eventual transition to the new space, sounding world weary and depressing as he could.

As we left the conference room both dejected and pissed off, Klein managed to pull myself and Azov aside into a smaller conference room.

"Listen , I could tell you were losing it in there Chris. Everything I just said was for Berg's benefit. I just want him to think that and I also want him to stop constantly asking for favors. You do realize that correct?"

Azov broke into a knowing smile. I, on the other hand, didn't really see the difference between his fake meeting and the very real effect it was having on the team.

145   ©2015

"Whatever Steve, in the future, count me out of the fake meetings ok?" I spat out.

"Waaait Chris...C'mon, we're all in the circle of trust here. Don't step outside the circle!"

"Step outside the circle of mistrust? I'll make sure I keep an eye out for that" I said.

I had had enough of his crap. I had brought in enough business that he couldn't afford to fire me without wounding the department. I wasn't one to throw my weight around, but this was utterly ridiculous.

"Hey...enough with the insubordination. Show a little respect." Klein said

"Yes sir, very sorry sir, I'll make sure I attend all fake meetings in the future." I said mockingly.

"C'mon Chris, come over to my desk and I'll show you where everybody is going to be sitting. You'll like your new spot. Jim and I have been working on this and you are going to be far away from Berg. Omar will have the privilege of sitting directly next to him." Klein said, trying to mollify me in his own weak way, while letting me know Omar was being punished.

©2015

Klein knew he had pushed it too far with me, that I was calling into question vocally what everyone else was thinking. He couldn't fire me, and he couldn't promote me. Sharetech was too big for that, and a process had to be followed. Corporate certainly hadn't empowered him with that type of additional authority given his track record thus far.

As such, I felt at ease to let him know I was only playing along because it made things easier, not because I was worried that he could do anything to me. Klein was only 5 years older me, not 15, so I didn't view standing up to him as crossing someone my father's age. To me, it was more like the nerdiest kid I knew in High School had gone on some demented power trip and was working out serious issues with the 3 of us as his laugh track and Berg as the chief object of his locker room torture. The fact that Steve was so well versed in this behavior led me to believe that he had probably been the victim of it himself in the past.

Day 220- We have recently moved into our shiny new offices on a high floor overlooking the Hudson river in Jersey City. The view was spectacular. Our floor contained roughly 250 people over a wide area "cubicle farm".

 ©2015

Klein had taken up his seat and resumed his usual personal phone calls to whomever it was he spoke to on the phone for hours every day. He clearly had not realized how much his speech and behavior had degenerated during our time in the "Walking Dead" office across the street. He was loudly dropping F bombs as usual, and now everyone in the room was witness to hearing this at 8:30a. Klein always got in early, and he immediately began drawing looks from people who thought he was nuts.

Klein failed to understand that a big part of working for a large company in corporate America is a 'flattening' of those aspects of one's personality that might be perceived as risky or out of bounds. Personality quirks were viewed as having far more risk than reward in an age of rigidly enforced rules designed to limit liability and risk. This conformity served a purpose; to help eliminate conflicts and theoretically promote cohesion, albeit one that carried with it the implied threat of disciplinary action. Nevertheless, the net result was that you rarely heard outbursts, foul language, or any histrionics of any type as I had witnessed at smaller firms I had worked at though the years. It may have been boring, but it

  ©2015

was safe and predictable, and that is what publicly traded companies liked.

However, Klein was more oblivious to this concept than ever. He and Berg each seemed to share their own delusional bubble of how their behavior appeared to others. His time across the street only heightened aspects of his personality that fingered him as a potentially strange and hostile co-worker.

Unfortunately, this, along with his non-stop insistence that everyone hated us and resented our presence on the floor, only served to create a self-fulfilling prophecy. We became known as "the guys who worked with that loud guy who swears on the phone all the time". In the absence of any real information, speculation usually filled the gap.

Needless to say, Steve was hardly an ambassador of goodwill for our department to the rest of the floor, or the rest of the company, and the HR department knew this better than we were aware of.

 ©2015

Day 265- Another day, another torturous staff meeting with Klein. We all took our seats for another one of his interminable "smack down" sessions, where he alternated between painting a dark picture of us as a department, of the industry in general and then basically opposed everything that Berg said to him. The more Klein opposed him, the more Berg had to say...so it often devolved into a back and forth, tit for tat of thinly veiled hostility with Azov and Omar snickering and myself staring out the window trying to visualize myself far away from this room and it's petty battles.

Today however, we received word from Klein that we had been summoned by HR for a multi-day training seminar.

"So HR has decided to send us to a training, which you will all be getting an email about, called Dysfunctions of a Group: How to Overcome Group Dysfunction and Find Success" Klein said in a monotone voice.

Apparently, corporate was officially "on to us" and what was going on.

Later on that day after the meeting with everybody, Klein pulled myself and Azov, aside into

©2015

a small conference room. I often wondered how the other two felt about this as we all officially held the same title as they did, but we were clearly treated differently as members of the so-called "inner circle".

"Ok, so listen, we have to go to this bullshit corporate retraining crap blah blah blah, and I actually view it as a positive." Klein exhaled in a tired way.

Jim, sounding appropriately exasperated, said "Really, how can this be viewed of as a positive?"

What followed next seems like it should have been predictable, but also stretches to the outer reaches of bizarre.

"It'll be the perfect way to blame all these problems on Berg. Everybody knows these problems are his fault, that he is constantly creating trouble" Klein said.

Actually, that was all true........about Steve Klein. Klein, however, never allowed himself to see any of this. His hatred and vindictiveness for Berg was so all consuming, it appeared to be the only reason he woke up in the morning. I looked at Jim, who was appearing to listen to Klein as he spoke, but when he could, gave me a side glance very

    ©2015

quickly. He was better at containing his incredulity than I was, perhaps perceiving Klein as a future job connection or reference, he was always in control of his response to whatever brand of crazy Klein happened to spewing at a given moment. Clearly a better man than I.

I, on the other hand, piped up a bit.

"Steve, this can't really be good for us...." He immediately cut me off

"It'll be fine, don't worry about it, you are always so worried about that stuff......I got this under control. I am not going to be super obvious how I go about this...I know what these people want to hear and the whole thing will blow over." Klein said.

Klein's considerable talent for denial was in full force.

It sounded very much like he was convincing himself while also attempting to convince us. Given the circumstances, I had a strong feeling that neither was remotely successful.

©2015

Day 272- Today was the meeting with the so-called "group facilitator" who was going to lead the "Dysfunctions of a group" remedial training seminar. She apparently had come in from the US company headquarters in Boston to share this wonderful day with us.

"Hello, my name is Rebecca Maslow, and I am with the HR personnel evaluation and remediation department in Boston. I am here today to help facilitate the "Dysfunctions of a group" seminar to try and help understand how we can work together and more efficiently while also understanding each others differences and boundaries as they relate to a healthy professional work environment" she said.

Around the conference table were several packets of paper ensconced in a folder with the corporate logo on it. As I opened my folder, the title page had a picture of some phony looking people in business casual outfits sitting around a cubicle farm with maniacal grins on their faces, laughing. Above this picture the title 'Dysfunctions of a Group: Understanding Group Dysfunctions and How to Improve Communication and Productivity'.

The whole thing was depressing to say the least, because as a group, our goal of producing business

  ©2015

was actually going quite well. However, Steve Klein's goal of ostracizing Mitch Berg to the point of quitting or worse, overshadowed everything and threatened to bring down the entire department. I know I've said this many times before, but it bears repeating.

We all saw this HR bullshit for what it was...a warning from corporate that the appropriate steps were being taken to begin rooting out and understanding where the trouble was coming from. The numerous meetings that Berg and Klein had with HR, as well as the truancy and lack of production of Omar, were now showing up on the HR departments radar as well as those of Klein's immediate superior, Andrew. They didn't know exactly what was going on, but they knew trouble had been brewing for quite some time.

This is what big companies did when they were beginning the process of getting rid of people. My fear was that they might throw me out with everybody else, that I would become swept up in the current of negativity and lumped in with the main offenders.

From a corporate viewpoint, Berg, Klein and Ahmedy all represented potential lawsuits against the company. This wasn't speculation, but, from

   ©2015

what I had heard as rumor from Azov, an overt threat that had been made by Berg as a response to Klein's ceaseless harassment. I had heard Omar mention the same possibility himself to me on walks to the train, citing discrimination for his lack of production and timely work performance.

While none of these supposed lawsuits seemed to have any real merit, from the company's perspective it didn't matter. The very filing of a lawsuit cost money to defend, and so, here we were at the company's attempt to remedy the situation. At the very least, they would be able to make the claim that they had tried to understand what was going on with this seminar if this ever did end up as a legal case.

"Ok, if everyone could please take the next 30 minutes or so to read the materials I just passed out and then sign the last page of everything in front of you, then I will come back in and we will discuss and introduce ourselves and see if we can't gain a little understanding as what is going on and how we can move forward." Rebecca said

With that she left the room and shut the door, and all five of us were left staring at each other around the table. With Berg in the room, the tension was so dense you felt as though could

 ©2015

almost touch it. We all opened our books and began reading. Of course, Berg could never handle silence for long, and always felt it was better to say something inane, nonsensical or annoying then say nothing at all.

"Oh great, some light reading" he blurted out. Silence.

"What a load of bullshit.." Omar muttered under his breath.

"Let's just be quiet and try and get through this so we can go upstairs and get back to work." Klein said, doing his best impression of a semi-competent manager.

About a half hour later, Rebecca reemerged into the room with a saccharin smile on her face. Apparently she had drank several sips of the Kool-Aid.

"Ok, did everybody get through the booklet and the exercises?" A discernible low grumble went through the room followed by Mitch blurting out "Yes! I did!!" as loud as he could.

The exercises contained in the book were really just us rating the effectiveness of our department in our own opinion on a scale of 1 to 5. 5 was the

©2015

most positive. Needless to say none of my ratings were very good, and I would assume that was the case for others as well.

Rebecca, who didn't seem to really have much to say outside of the prescribed curriculum for this little project, opened the book and asked us, one by one, to recite our reactions to the statement "Our group often works proactively together to solve problems in a positive way"

Klein spoke up first, eager to fire the opening salvo.

"I think that as a group, most of us do work together well....ahh.....but that certain members, blah blah blah, of the group feel that they aren't team players and that they should get special consideration that gives them a different set of rules than everybody else."

His constant use of "blah blah blah" immediately undermined any meaning the sentence may have had. I looked around the room and saw Berg turning red as a vein popped out of his neck.

"Would anybody else in the group like a chance to expand on that?" Rebecca stated.

157 ©2015

For a moment there was silence, as everybody tried to assess what to do and the best course of action to take. It was very much a no-win scenario. Everybody knew what the real problem was, but nobody was going to be the guy to point the finger. At the end of this exercise, we all knew that we had to go back upstairs and deal with each other no matter what the outcome of this session was.

"I'd say that people probably just need to communicate a little more openly" Jim opened up with his most reasonable sounding general comment he could think of. This was a small victory for all of us, given the circumstances.

"It's hard to argue with that Jim, and I'd say that is a good start. Does anyone else have anything they'd like to add to that" Rebecca said.

She was clearly just going through the motions and checking the boxes appropriately for this exercise. Or maybe she was smart enough to not wade into the middle of a nasty dog fight.

"I agree with Jim, but I'd also like to say that certain members of the team need to think of themselves as a part of a team, and realize that

©2015

they aren't above anyone else or better than anyone else." Steve offered.

This was clearly another jab at Berg. While it was true that Berg was not only weak at his job, he was also a caustic mix of ambition, self-loathing, pathos and ego. His bitterness over the longstanding "manager" title and his manager "override" that he had never received was also always front and center in his mind. He held onto this thought as it was some type of gold bauble that must be cherished, despite the fact he would never actually receive either.

Apparently before I had started, according to what Jim had told me, he had gone up to a senior level executive to lobby for his "override" after being on the job less than two months. The executive, who had no idea who he was or what he did, politely backed out of the conversation and reported it to Klein's superior Andrew. Needless to say, the political fallout was substantial for Klein. This was the genesis for Berg and Klein not getting along.

The fact that the next person hired, Jim, essentially assumed this role of manager from Mitch, despite being 20 years his junior was perceived as an egregious affront by Berg. Never

 ©2015

mind the fact that Berg neither had the temperament, attitude, or competence for the manager role. In his mind, he was screwed by Klein, and this made him all the more selfishly motivated to try and angle back to getting what he perceived was his proper place within the division. If he thought he could accomplish this through ham-handed attempts at HR meetings or strange manipulative behavior, he was going to try it.

All of this only served to alienate Berg not only from Klein, which was a given, but also from the rest of the team, many of whom were people like myself who may have had some sympathy for him if he wasn't so hell bent on making sure they didn't.

All of these thoughts went through my head for the one hundredth time as this inane "Dysfunctions of a Group" training droned on. Nobody was going to really say anything of substance as this Rebecca person went through the exercises in the book and wrapped up the phony 'action plan' for our department.

We knew what the problem was, and the company was trying to find out what and who was at fault, the manager, the employee or both. However,

©2015

none of us saw one shred of benefit to helping the company figure out what was going on, because we had all been through scenarios where the company inevitably swept up the so-called whistleblower into the situation as well.

In short, nobody could really be trusted.

As the meeting drew to its predictably dreary and unsatisfying conclusion, we all knew that there was no such thing as a neutral bystander in the shit storm we found ourselves in the middle of. The situation seemed like it was going to play out to its logical conclusion, one way or another.

Day 285 – Steve wasn't in today, and he sent myself and Jim an email saying that he was dealing with his ailing father, who was 91 years old and was close to death. He told us he would be in and out intermittently over the next few days depending on what happened. He didn't bother to include his former 'favorite guy' Omar on these emails anymore. He had been 'excommunicated' for poor sales performance, showing up late almost constantly and generally not even bothering to make a show of being motivated.

Not having Klein in the office was a relief, as we could all take a break from his constant calling us

    ©2015

over to his desk for some strange internet stalking he had done, or hear his latest plot against Berg..or hear some bizarre "Fuck that!" echoing forth from his desk. Usually when that happened we all sort of slumped down in our cubicles, as if the embarrassing drunk Uncle we wished we didn't know was acting up again in front of the 50 other employees in our immediate vicinity who knew very little about us, except that we had an insane and vulgar manager.

Berg, never being one to leave well enough alone , often used the opportunity of Klein not being in the office as an immediate reason to start being louder and more phonily "chipper" than he normally was. How this often translated is that he would come over to our cubicles, ask a phony leading question to start a conversation, and then would slowly turn the conversation into him trying to extract information about something he wanted to know, usually concerning his job, money, or something about Steve that could be potentially used to incriminate him in the HR battle between them.

Essentially, he would go on a 'fact-finding' mission around to all of us, under the guise of being 'one of the guys' which was just another performance

162   ©2015

he could not convincingly pull off. He wouldn't do this when Klein was in the office because he was too paranoid that Klein was watching his every move for the slightest misstep. This assessment was 100% correct, but it took all his discipline to not walk around babbling to people because it was always his nature to talk more, not less...and every conversation had the capacity to become a time bomb where he would say something very abrasive, awkward or impolite....or all three.

Of course, Jim, myself and Omar saw this coming from him a mile away. In the beginning, we used to try and engage him like a normal human coworker. However, we all quickly saw thru his annoying ruse, and realized he had no interest in anything we were going to say that didn't satisfy what he perceived as his interests....

Eventually, this led us to where we were today. Often, we would see him coming, and could accurately predict what angle of fake questioning he was going to try and take with us. Then, we would make up completely false answers that would play straight into his pre-existing anxieties.

It may not have been nice, but we felt we were justified, and it was entertaining to watch his head spin as he tried to fathom the results. Plus

 ©2015

our own moral compasses were so skewed at this point it seemed normal to us.

Today, Omar happened on the idea of coming up with an entirely fake lead that would be posed as a huge company looking to take advantage of our services. This was an expanded variation on the ploy that had been cooked up months ago with Klein in the bar.

Because our phones were connected to an 800 number that rang at all of our desks in a "hunt" pattern for inbound calls, the call could be made to go to someone other than Berg. Because Berg always obsessively watched what everyone else was doing so he could judge how it might hurt or help him, he would immediately find out about it (especially if Omar wanted him to) and it would be revealed that it was a huge client he had missed out on because he was away from his desk for 5 minutes.

"Dude it will drive him nuts that he missed this." Omar said.

"Oh my god...it's genius. He sits at his desk close to 8 hours a day waiting for once a month chance call that may come in, and the minute he goes to

©2015

the bathroom he misses the 'whale' and it goes to one of us." I said.

We all laughed together as we gamed out how "big" we wanted to make this "lead"without it becoming totally outlandish.

"Ok so I say we give it some real generic name like Gannet Industries, and make sure that it has like 8000 locations and does over $1bn per year in sales." Azov said

"Chris, you got to be the one to book this sale, I can have a friend call in from outside and Berg can overhear you talking about it on the line." We had perfected this routine since the night at the bar with Klein over a year ago.

However, I knew better than to get involved directly. Berg was dangerous, and my educated guess was that he cast a very wide net with HR in trying to incriminate the entire department in being against him and part of Klein's conspiracy, despite the fact this may very well make him look insane. I didn't want to make that situation worse, and had no interest in ending up in a meeting with HR to discuss this lunacy, as funny as it may have been. To me, it wasn't worth it.

 ©2015

"Sorry guys, it'll have to be someone else, can't do it." I said

"Cmon Chris, he already is jealous of you and this would make it worse...he'll be going nuts over it" Omar said

"Can't do it...I don't want to end up in Berg's little black list of grievances that he keeps in his drawer." I responded, only half-joking, as we were fairly certain such a list existed.

"Too late...I'm sure we are all already in there!" Azov said. He was right, but I didn't need to add insult to injury, or make it worse than it already was.

"Sorry...love the idea but one of you guys is going to have to do it yourself. Plus I don't want to have to listen to him interrogate me about it. Are you guys going to put it on the monthly sales report? If so, you better be careful...."

Knowing Berg, he may take a picture of the Excel list we kept our monthly report on and then try to go to HR saying people were falsifying documents on company property or some similar type of complaint to try and bring as many people down with him as possible if the joke somehow went bad or he found out.

  ©2015

"Thats a good point, we better try and keep the whole thing to a series of phone conversations that he overhears. Otherwise it could get a little dangerous. No documentation." Azov said.

"I know just the guy who can help us with this, a buddy of mine who already knows about Berg and has heard the stories." Azov continued.

And so the caper went forward, with predictable results. Berg found out about the new "client", immediately walked over to Azov's desk and started interrogating where it came from, how it came in, how big it was, when he was going to put it on the monthly sales report on the shared drive, etc. Once he got those particulars, you always got a phony "Congratulations!!" that barely masked any bitterness Berg had for not signing the client himself.

He then would return to his seat and sit silently staring at his computer, sometimes for over an hour, churning and stewing in his own head. After he had done this, he then came over to Azov's desk again with a new angle of questioning.

"Why isn't Gannet industries on the monthly report yet for this month?" Berg asked, with a

©2015

particularly acid tone in his voice, at once both urgent and peeved.

"I just haven't added it yet, but I will, don't worry." said Azov, doing his best impression of a cool cucumber, not even looking up from his computer. Berg just stood over Azov's cubicle and stared for awhile, Azov looked up at him and stared back...then Berg finally turned and went back to his desk, seemingly at a loss for words for what seemed like the first time in his entire life.

Even when Klein wasn't in the office, it seems as though he had managed to train all of us to act in his image...and none of us even really realized it anymore.

Day 300 - We got word today from Steve that his Dad had died. This word came by way of an email to Jim, which was also forwarded to me.

The email gave the basics of the funeral & memorial arrangements, letting us know that we didn't have to attend if we did not want to. However, even for this solemn occasion, the battle with Berg could not be put aside.

 ©2015

I read the email that Klein had written in response to me objecting to him ordering us not to tell Berg about the funeral. The main thrust of what I had said was that if he didn't want Berg to go to his Dad's funeral, that was his call, but he shouldn't put us, as his co-workers, in the position of being the people to tell him that. I thought that should've come directly from Steve as the manager.

Klein's email reply to me was both astonishing and chilling. Or at least it was to me.

"My father was well aware of what Berg did to me in going to HR and he would not have wanted him at his funeral. I know Berg's type…. he would jump all over the chance to be at the funeral, he is into that stuff. What I do know is this, my father would not have wanted him there. There is no reason he needs to know about my dad, as I am telling all of you to keep quiet about it. I will tell him what happened after the fact when I return to work. If it does turn out that he happens to show up at the funeral, I will have him escorted out of the building immediately. My fathers memorial service is by invite-only and you, Omar and Jim are invited, but no Mitch Berg under any circumstances."

 ©2015

The idea that his father, who was past 90 and apparently a very accomplished person, was part and parcel to the petty conflicts Klein was having at work was incredible to me. For all I know, it may not have been true, but just Klein's imagination or perhaps his wish.

My own father had passed many decades before, and I tried to place myself into Klein's shoes and attempt to understand how he could bring his recently passed father into this...and tie his passing into the conflict with Berg. The passing of ones parent is often a time of reflection, but not for Klein. For him, it was an opportunity to continue what he had been doing all along. It showed the depths that he was sinking to...the fact that writing an email like that seemed normal, or even justified to him was a stark example of his warped perspective.

The even stranger part about this bitter email, was that there was an element of truth in it.

It was true that Berg had been asking about Klein's dad almost daily as soon as he learned his health was failing, fishing for information. Myself and Azov were sworn to secrecy, having to explain Klein's many recent absences by stating that we had no idea where he was. Of course, Berg knew

©2015

this wasn't the case and he knew that we knew where Klein was...but we weren't saying anything. Berg only knew that Klein's dad was elderly and had been ill for sometime, but that was it. However, he highly suspected that something was up regarding his health.

I also knew that no matter how much Berg resented or hated Klein for the unending torture they put each other through daily, he would indeed show up at his Dad's funeral if he found out, whether he was invited or not, just to piss Klein off and essentially challenge Klein to make himself look bad by throwing him out of the service.

It had absolutely nothing to do Berg's respect for the dead, or a sincere desire to bury the hatchet for even a moment, but that would be how he played it, even if he wasn't invited. If there was one thing that Berg really enjoyed, it was being a total noodge, a contrarian who enjoyed doing the opposite of what people wanted or expected and then playing it totally straight like he had no idea he was doing it, just to piss people off.

That kind of "noodginess" was part of his everyday routine. It was part of the reason why he refused to "learn computers" or get a cell phone that was

 ©2015

less then 15 yrs old. He liked the fact people thought he was strange and ask him about these things, and then he would go on a five minute rant or debate about his worldview that justified these things as though they were some sort of manifesto of common sense that the rest of the world just hadn't caught up with yet.

Meanwhile, the entire department was in the uncomfortable position of knowing that Klein's father had died, but unable to say anything to Berg, despite his insistent questioning that grew increasingly pointed with each passing day of Klein's absence.

Day 303 - It turns out that Klein's father had his memorial service this Sunday. The three of us, minus Berg, decided to attend not only out of sympathy, but also out of respect for our boss, and most importantly, for political reasons. Having respect for Klein was mostly a simulated, or virtual affair on all three of our parts. As for Berg, he clearly didn't believe in faking it.

Because I had been out of work so long prior to this job, many of the material things that go into a life had begun to fray badly. The house, the car,

  ©2015

the wardrobe, all suffered from a lot of maintenance that had been deferred in the interest of eating, keeping the kids in decent clothes, and paying the mortgage.

As such, I found myself driving to Steves' fathers' service out on Long Island in my 9 year old car that had well over 120,000 miles on it. Prior to the economic crash, it had been serviced fairly regularly, but I began to hear a strange sound on the way there and then realized once I had stopped for gas that the car would barely start.

I arrived at the memorial service early and parked far out in the parking lot, knowing that if I turned the car off, it may not start again and also knowing I could not afford what would surely be a 400 dollar tow the 60 miles back to my New Jersey neighborhood.

After much mental handwringing, I made the call to leave the car running, taking a chance that it would not be stolen. Given that I was in a neighborhood full of Mercedes, BMW's, I was fairly certain nobody wanted a used 9 year old Honda.

Upon walking into the memorial service prior to its start, I saw Omar and Jim, and the three of us greeted Klein, keeping the conversation light and

173   ©2015

focused on the moment at hand. We all donned our Yarmulkes out of respect and were seated in the congregation.

The first thing that struck me, as a veteran of many funerals, was a large portrait sized picture of Steve's father surrounded by three Golden Retrievers. His father had a huge smile on his face, and the dogs certainly seemed to be smiling as well.

At once I thought it was both nice, and a little strange. Clearly, the dogs were not at the memorial service, only his family was. I couldn't decide if I was reading something into this or perhaps it actually was a little odd that the one picture they chose to display and represent their dad was one that didn't include any humans or family members.

I brushed it off as over-analyzing on my part, but as it turns out, my instincts may have been more correct than I imagined.

The service began with the Rabbi saying a few kind and wise words about the deceased. It was then the turn of family members to speak. Steve was the first up, as one of the two of elder twins to speak.

   ©2015

"Hello, my name is Steve Klein, and I am the son of Seth Klein. I've never been one for sentimentality of any kind, so I've prepared something to give you an idea of what my dad did during his life and what he accomplished." Steve stated flatly.

What followed was a laundry list of impressive accomplishments in the fashion and construction industries that was dry and encyclopedic in its reading. Steve read this 5 minute speech in a emotionless and monotone voice, with no evidence of stress. He then finished his speech in the same routine manner and handed the podium over to his twin brother, who looked significantly different than he did.

His twin brother gave an engaging and emotional overview of their relationship and what it meant to him, highlighting a few of the more touching moments in their time together through the decades. In short, it seemed a lot more like what one might expect to hear a son saying about his father.

The other speakers over the course of the next hour, brothers, a wife, daughters, uncles....did the same. In the end, Steve's speech stood out for everything that it wasn't...which was the least bit

 ©2015

sentimental, or even emotional on any level. It was merely a recitation of facts. I came to start thinking that perhaps in Steve's mind, he thought that this was how his Dad wanted it. Perhaps he thought this was a way of giving his Dad credit for all he had done, and that he felt his Dad wanted this credit.

My conclusion was that perhaps this was an insight into their relationship, and by extension, the issue at hand with Berg, and perhaps many other people Klein had come into contact with during the course of his life.

Maybe it was an insight...and maybe it wasn't. But I came away feeling I had learned something about Steve Klein. The something I had learned didn't seem to be anything he was aware of, and therefore,it was probably something that could never be fixed. And this thing, this aspect that now seemed obvious to me, was not good.....not good at all for anybody that had any extended dealings with Steve Klein

 ©2015

And just like that he was gone....no more, no longer with us. All we were left with was the money and the fighting. And that was fine by me. I would get up and say my piece, and do my best to let the whole world know what he always wanted it to know. That he was the best, that he achieved more than most for the things he cared about.

The people he made money for, the people who worked for him, his family, his dogs...they all owed him...and he loved it. I would let everyone know how well he did. Because when people owed you, you owned them. He liked that...a lot.

But I'd be damned if I was going to show him, my Dad, or anyone else who ever knew him, one ounce of regret at his passing...one ounce of sadness. I had already done that while he was alive. Now that he was gone...sadness wasn't even an option. Those feelings had evaporated many decades ago, replaced by the hard reality of how my father viewed me, how he viewed my brother, and how he viewed just about everyone else.

I'd give him his goddamn public reading of his list of achievements. Name, rank and serial number only. If there was anything that he had taught me, its that blubbering in front of people, whether

177   ©2015

they were strangers, family or friends, was always a losing gambit. I certainly wasn't going to start now that he had died.

Of course my brother got up there and choked back tears, as the perfect son he always was, and the picture of him and the dogs stood in silent, smirking testament to the fact my father showed more love to those animals than any other living thing on earth. Nobody said this out loud, except for me in a different time and place. For that I was quickly shouted down. Anyone I may have said that to owed him too much to challenge the dominant narrative he was selling.

My father praised loyalty over all else. Thats why the dogs were always at the top of his personal food chain. I suppose thats what people who fear their own behavior and actions tend to do. Keep my secrets and you'll be rewarded....keep my secrets....or else. My father's calculation on life was taught to me early on. You make the money, you do what you have to do, and you buy everyone's silence and complacence. It didn't matter who they were...your friends, your family, your employees....he knew that everyone could be bought, and the whole thing was sealed up in that lovely word he used so often: loyalty. Loyalty

©2015

above judgement, morality, decency…..there was a reason the mafia movies always talked about it.

But somehow I never fit into that. I was the proverbial red-headed step child, even though I was a twin. My father didn't understand me, and that which he didn't understand...he often didn't approve of. Let's face it, he didn't want to acknowledge the fact that we were related at all..as if I was a some sort of ugly distorted mirror that caused him self loathing, caused him to, no matter how briefly, question himself. The fact that I never responded to what he thought was motivation, well that made it even worse.

I'll find my way though....now that he is gone there is one lesson that I clearly learned. That when someone does you wrong, when they break your loyalty, when they step outside the circle....they must be made to pay. Made to pay, so that they will never make that mistake again and forever regret the day they did.

©2015

Day 317- The funeral behind us, Steve had returned to work. He somehow never had managed to tell Berg one thing that happened. As far as Berg was concerned, Klein's father was still alive.

All of us were told not to tell him, that Klein would handle it. Over the past 10 days, and in the wake of the "Dysfunctions of a Group" corporate problem solving seminar, a meeting was called.

For a change, this one didn't appear to be a sham designed to torture Berg to ever higher degrees. We all went into the conference room and Klein sat down in his usual laconic and tired manner. He loved to bring a depressing pall into the room, and for a normal person, I would've said that he was grieving over his father. However, I knew that this wasn't the reason because he had been trying to make meetings as depressing and painful as possible for a long time...as those of you who have read this diary already know.

"Ok...ahhh...so Andrew wanted me to call everyone together...blah blah blah.... today to let you know of some changes occurring in the department. Effective immediately, I am no longer your manager. That is going to be handled by Roberta Jenkins. So you will go to her for HR issues,

 ©2015

scheduling PTO...blah blah blah. In terms of the business side of things, sales, leads...I am still in charge of that. So nothing has really changed except that you go to her to schedule time off, things like that." Steve was actively selling that this was no big deal, which almost certainly guaranteed that it was.

Berg could barely contain his glee and immediately piped up.

"So, (nervous throat clearing), this means that if I have any HR issues, if I want to schedule time off or have other issues I report directly to Roberta and no longer you?"

Berg was slowly twisting the knife now...the battle could never be paused, not for a millisecond. The use of the phrase "report to" was definitely a calculated move to throw it right in Steve's face.

"No Mitch, thats not what I said. You still report to me regarding anything about business matters, sales figures and your performance review will be filled out by me and signed off on by Roberta. You ONLY go to her if you need to schedule time off... blah blah...etc or if you have some type of HR issue you need to discuss with her that can't be handled

 ©2015

internally." Klein said, clearly bored with this already.

"Right exactly, but I technically report to Roberta about anything not sales related, and she also signs off on my performance review..." Mitch said, pressing in his tone and body language.

"She signs off on the performance review AFTER I complete my input...she is basically going to do whatever I say regarding your sales performance..." Klein said.

"So wait, I don't understand, Roberta signs off on whatever you write? Or she has to approve it? I'm just asking because I'm not clear what the difference is.(nervous throat clearing)"

Berg was really enjoying this now. As was always the case with him, if you gave him the smallest opening, if you opened the door just a crack, he would burst through it and usually over-exploit whatever imaginary advantage he felt he had.

"I think I made myself very clear Mitch...." Klein went on while Berg interrupted him again.

"Ok,(throat clear) well maybe I'll just ask Roberta then because it's pretty important that I understand exactly who I report to."

182

©2015

Klein was perturbed, but still in control of himself enough to continue jabbing Berg.

"Mitch, it's real simple. For anything sales or business related you go to me, for anything else, you go to Roberta. Understand?'

Berg wasn't quite ready to let this go, a few more turns of the screw would be necessary to extract his pound of flesh in his moment of "victory".

"So then you will be doing our performance review or will Roberta? I'm still unclear."

Klein, with a sharp edged, deliberate tone, went on.

"I will be writing the comments as your manager and Roberta will be signing off on them before it gets sent up to Andrew for final review"

This seemed to satisfy Berg, because he now thought that he was going to get a fair shake in the corporate review process. It was not a stretch at all to say that this was a continuing pain point in their ongoing HR battle, and I am sure that his review from Steve was always skewed in the most negative way.

   ©2015

To make matters trickier for Berg, the only person, up until this moment, who could supersede Steve Klein's performance review was Klein's boss, Andrew, who was in the California office 3000 miles away. To say that Andrew was out of the loop was an understatement. This was partially what had allowed for an overpaid attorney like Klein to turn the department into his personal vendetta machine against one of his own.

However, now a new dynamic was in force. Essentially, Klein had been given a babysitter by the company. A trusted executive who was in charge of over 600 people and had 20 years of experience was now going to "bear witness" to whatever was going on within our department close up. Apparently, if the kids couldn't manage themselves, a "parent" would be brought in to make sure things were being handled in the right way.

It was all very embarrassing. Myself, Azov and Ahmedy all felt ashamed to be part of such a charade. We also knew that on some level, we had become complicit in Kleins bad behavior, partially out of a dislike for Berg and his own insane selfish antics, partially out of concern for our jobs...and partially because our own vindictiveness and

©2015

darkness had been encouraged to grow and flourish under Klein and his unending plots within plots to hamstring and torture Berg.

And for his part, Berg took all his cues from Klein as well as he sought conflict and was ultimately trying to win by getting Klein fired. It was clearly a battle to the death, if not literally, certainly in a figurative sense. Though there were times I wasn't sure about which was which.

Regardless, this meeting was actually a preview of the "official" introduction to Roberta. In most cases, Klein had sought to severely limit our contact with the rest of the company, and this was our first venture out of our hermetically sealed bubble. In some ways, I was looking forward to it. I was desperate for any measure that would end this insanity that passed for a work experience.

The next day, Thursday, we were introduced to Roberta Jenkins.

She seemed very level headed and was polite but basically non-committal. She didn't pretend to know everything that was going on, but I have no doubt she was thoroughly briefed on the personnel situation by HR. After managing that many employees, this probably was a fairly standard

 ©2015

situation for her to be in, and that no doubt played a big role in why she was chosen.

She left the meeting letting us know what to expect in terms of timing and deadlines for her HR stuff, and also let us know that her door was always open. Somehow,when she said it, I actually believed her.

That was all Berg needed to hear, and his hand popped up immediately to speak to her after the meeting.

I'm sure that he wanted to get on her schedule as quickly as possible to begin making his case against Klein.

 ©2015

Day 335 As I sat at my terminal, sending out emails to clients and prospects, I received an email that caused me to stop in my tracks.

"Hi Chris, Barbara here in HR. Could you please stop down on the 27th floor for a short chat? I wanted to go over something with you real quick. No need to mention this to anybody.

Thanks,
Barb"

I sat silent for a moment, trying to think of anything I might have done that would cause me to get called down there. I drew a blank, except for some extremely paranoid scenarios that really didn't seem make any sense at all. I then began to think of all the ways this could blow back on me.

If I went down to Barbara's office without telling Klein and he found out about it, which I had to assume he would, he would immediately accuse me of being disloyal and a part of the "the company assholes who are out to get him". If I did tell him that I was going down there, he would probably pump me for information about the

187   ©2015

meeting afterward, a meeting that was surely going to be labelled "confidential" by Barb.

Because I still had little confidence the company would ever take any concrete steps to stop Klein and Berg from their increasingly acidic confrontations, despite the addition of Roberta, I really couldn't count on anyone to be my ally. I had to remember my first concern, which was to stay clear of trouble and keep my job. I had covered the business end of that three sided equation, but I had no idea coming into this that this would actually be the easiest part of it.

I chose to tell Klein that I was going down to visit HR

"Steve, I just got an email from HR, they want me to go down there."

"What? What do they want you to go down there for?" Klein looked up, eyes darting about.

"I don't know, they didn't say, I'm assuming its about you and Berg, but it could be anything. I just wanted you to know what was going on."

"You better not do anything to fuck me. Remember the circle of trust. Don't tell them shit, or just let them know it's Bergs fault." Steve said.

188   ©2015

Yeah, ok....thanks a lot Steve.

Of course, this is exactly what I knew he would do. I was also pretty sure that anything I did, short of being totally silent in the room, would be interpreted by Klein as "fucking him over" and being disloyal. That was the lens his increasingly paranoid and demented mindset saw everything through. The only person who was usually beyond reproach was his favorite Jim, but lately even he was starting to crack under the pressure, and had had a few words with Klein letting him know he was crossing the line, if such a line still existed.

Klein knew the walls were closing in, but he was merely upping his bravado to mask any nervousness he may have felt. Lately, he was constantly mentioning his Ivy League degree, his wealth and the stupidity, ignorance and cheapness of the company. He also had told us that he was, in the midst of the shit storm he had essentially created, attempting to renegotiate his employment contract for a higher salary. He certainly didn't lack for brazen Chutzpah.

I stepped out into the hallway after having the pressure loaded on my shoulders by Klein. I felt very much like events were spinning out of control, and that I was being caught up in the

189   ©2015

undertow. I really didn't see any positive outcome to this upcoming meeting, and my goal was to walk into Barbara's office and say as little as I could get away with.

As the elevator door closed and took me down to Barbara's office, I thought of all the moments that had brought me to this one. It seemed that in my career, working hard had very little to do with whether success was achieved. Time and again, other peoples choices and actions had resulted in catastrophic results for the companies I had worked for that would, had we had lived in a logical world, would not have happened or been given such importance.

Regardless of this, I had to do my best to tread the very thin line that I now found myself walking. Whether this made any sense in the long run was really irrelevant. I had to do it now and hold onto any faith that this whole department wouldn't just implode in the coming days and weeks.

The elevator door opened and before I knew it, I was sitting in Barbara's office. The usual paper thin corporate pleasantries were exchanged, and I must have had a look on my face that said to her "get to the point". I was very unnerved to be

©2015

sitting in HR. It was like sitting in the principals office back in grammar school.

"Hi Chris. For starters I don't want you to worry... you are not in any trouble or anything like that, so you can relax." Barbara said.

I actually took this as a bad sign. Chalk it up to too many cop shows, but this sounded like something designed to get me to talk.

"The reason I called you down here is that there has been a lot of "noise" coming out of that department. To be honest, I'm not exactly sure what it is that you guys do, but it seems that there is a lot of noise and I thought maybe you could help us understand what is really going on in there."

Apparently "noise" was HR speak for "fucked up and dysfunctional" but I understood the necessity that euphemisms played in the situation.

"Why did you call me down? Did I do...." I started.

"No...no...no...not at all. Actually, that is why we called you down because you are the only person who doesn't really seem to be involved in what is going on up there and we thought that maybe you

          ©2015

could help us understand what is happening." she said.

Ok, so this is what I thought it was...an attempt to co-opt me as the snitch for corporate. Ain't gonna happen today lady...there was no upside for me to do that, and no motivation or assurances that it wouldn't negatively affect my job. I had no insight into Klein's status with the company, and as long as he was still my boss, I had to assume that he could manipulate the system to try and get me fired if he felt that I was disloyal or had "rolled over on him" to HR. While this would be very bad for him in any type of career sense, he had already shown an immense capacity for self destruction.

"Well, Ok, I'll try and do what I can...." I said weakly, giving the appearance of playing along.

"I just want you to know that anything we say here is held in complete confidence." Barbara said. Yeah right. Sure it is......... until it isn't.

"I understand, thanks for telling me." I said.

"Great. So do you see a lot of conflict between Steve and Mitch? Do you see Steve trying to insult Mitch in front of the group or the two of them arguing...any kind of conflict?"

©2015

"I mean, I do know that there is tension between them, but I can't say that I really see a lot of open conflict in front of me. I see them go into conference rooms a lot, but I have no idea what is being said in there or what takes place." I said, doing my best to sound matter-of-fact.

This was a total lie, but also plausible. Steve regaled myself and Azov with the stories of these private conference room confrontations with Berg on a regular basis, and seemed to delight in the fact that they made everyone involved miserable and stressed. He would actually call us over to his desk or ask us out to coffee at Starbucks so he could give us the play by play of the latest confrontation with Berg that he had had behind closed doors.

"So you don't see a lot going on or being initiated by Steve with regards to Mitch or anyone else?" she continued.

"Well, I know that Mitch has some problems with him and definitely has had issues in the past...."

"What about Steve, do you see him trying to provoke the situation with Mitch at all?"

"No I don't, but I can't speak to what is going on

 ©2015

behind closed doors or what is being said in their meetings. I do know they are in meetings a lot."

At this point I could see her face almost imperceptibly drop...she knew she wasn't going to get any good "red meat" information from me to help her investigation. In short order I was dismissed and the meeting was over.

"Thanks for your assistance with this, I just wanted to get your perspective on it."

"Not a problem Barbara, have a good day."

As I walked back down the long hallway to the elevator, my mind started churning. I couldn't believe what I had just witnessed, but then again, I had to. Not a lot of thought or concern was evident from HR as to how that exchange might have appeared to me. They apparently had their goal in mind, and they were going to give their ham handed attempt at getting me to talk a shot.

As the elevator dinged open back on my floor, I walked past the glass lined conference room and saw Jim and Steve inside. I wanted to keep walking, but Steve, knowing where I had just been, immediately called me in for a quick update.

    ©2015

"Ok Chris, spill the beans...what did you tell them?" Of course, he was suspicious.

"I wasn't down there very long, as you can tell. I didn't tell them anything really. What I can tell you is that you thought they were going to be talking to me about Berg, but mostly they wanted to know about you. I'm telling you Steve, they are coming for you so I would watch out."

This last part I meant sincerely. Despite everything, Klein and I had shared some good times outside of the office, and I knew that he had kids, just like I did. He needed to know that his actions were being noticed at the highest levels, and that he was in jeopardy. I also had a vague, almost quaint hope that it would curb his behavior. Of course, that would imply that his behavior was still within the bounds of his control.

"I can tell you told them something about me." was Kleins response, his vocal tone both searching and accusatory.

I laughed it off, and insisted I didn't, but he continued.

"Ooook Chris, I just hope you didn't step outside the circle."

   ©2015

I went back to my desk and sat there...my mind roiling. I started getting angry..and more angry. How dare Klein accuse of me of telling HR what he was really doing! What made it particularly infuriating was the fact that Azov and myself had done way more than Klein ever had to try and make the department a winner.

Klein was the epitome of a do nothing manager... he delegated almost every menial task to Azov, who essentially served as his secretary and right hand sales manager and administrator. This of course freed up more of his time for his revenge activities against Berg and internet stalking, two things that were often one in the same.

Within a very short period of time I had worked myself into a rage filled frenzy at the lunacy of this situation and the impossible position I was being put in. I was way past feeling sorry for myself and had moved right on to righteous indignation. I was quickly spiraling out of control as I felt my pulse quicken with anger.

Before long, Klein had finished his meeting and politely summoned me to the conference room, presumably for further debriefing. As I rose from my desk, I felt a fluttering of pure rage in my

 ©2015

chest and stomach and felt like I was about to explode.

The one thing I knew well about myself when I was feeling like this...the verbal stream that came out of my mouth was going to sting and cut very deeply...and I very well could've lost my job or, at the very least, been swept up in the HR maelstrom that I was trying so hard to swim against.

As I advanced closer and closer to the conference room, I saw Klein in there, with his smarmy grin and waiting eyes...dying to extract what he could from me while he simultaneously second guessing everything I told him.

I wasn't going in there.........I decided it right then.

There was no positive outcome that could occur from me going into that room. I kept walking right by the glass walled room, Klein looking at me with a quizzical look of disbelief.

I'm sure that the look on my face spoke volumes, but I kept going. I heard Steve call after me down the hallway, immediately knowing that something was wrong, and probably very worried about his own ass more than anything. I walked right out of the office into the hallway, Steve's calling voice coming after me.

 ©2015

I got on the elevator and went downstairs, taking deep breaths to calm myself down as I began sweating with the anger and rage that was flooding through my system. All I could think about was how this guy was trying to destroy everything and how that directly threatened my family...and it was as if he was doing it for entertainment, because he could...because he was gripped by a darkness that I could only fathom in the dimmest of ways.

Stepping through the revolving door and going outside, the spring air felt good, and the sunlight reminded me that there was so much more to this life than the lunacy that was inside the building. I felt like I could walk forever, and never see that place again. But I knew I could not do that, responsibility weighed on me and always quashed any thoughts of a dramatic exit.

At the same time, I was still severely agitated and walked directly to the bar down the street, not really knowing what else to do. I wasn't ready to go home in this state, as I would've been a mess in front of my family. As I was walking, I began to think that this was the most angry I had been in a very long time, perhaps going back decades to when I was a younger and more impulsive man.

 ©2015

I was taking Klein's assault on my livelihood, and that is exactly what it had evolved to be, very personally. And nobody was going to beat me personally, especially not a twisted fuck like him.

I walked into Monsignor Murphy's, the Irish pub about three blocks from the office, reeling internally but more or less in control. I quickly ordered a pint, and began drinking quicker than I normally would, waiting for the calming effects to kick in.

The TV's were on and the place had more than a few patrons, considering that it was only about 2:30p. The guy next to me appeared to have been there awhile as he was talking loudly and without the volume control customarily associated with sober people, informing everyone he was going to his job at 4p as a data cable contractor in one of the large office towers that surrounded the neighborhood.

As I looked up I saw they were broadcasting some type of foot race on TV. After a few minutes my phone rang and I knew it was Klein, worried about saving his ass, probably calling to try and talk me down. I was in no condition to talk to him as I was still on the edge of insanity and immediately pushed the call to voicemail.

 ©2015

I glanced up at the TV, taking another big swig of beer. Through the glass I could see there was smoke and chaos on the TV screen surrounding a large crowd of people at the foot race. A bloody figure was lying on the ground. It then became apparent that this was the Boston marathon and that a bomb had just gone off, severely injuring and killing people.

I drank my beer as despair washed over me and I turned away from the TV and the babbling, half-cocked idiot next to me.

Somehow, the chaos of the scene on TV and Klein's behavior were related in my mind at that moment. The only difference was the intensity and the degree of destruction involved. I felt ashamed to be a human as I sat there, wondering if there was ever any real solution to the scourge of our flawed construction. Perhaps we were all just lost in our own impossibly huge black room, with only the dimmest of flickering lights to find our way in the darkness, fumbling about blindly, causing our own catastrophe.......inch by inch by inch.

©2015

Day 335- The next day I decided to call in sick. I wasn't ready to go listen to Klein and his false apologies and whatever else he had to say. I just needed to get my head together and calm down and get ready to go back in there with poise and determination.

Once my emotions had subsided, I realized logically that things weren't quite as bleak as they had seemed. In my favor were excellent sales results, and this gave me some leverage. The key was to not overplay my hand or misuse it. I decided that to go back into the office with righteous indignation was the wrong move, because that would only cause Klein to become more defensive than he already was.

I spent that day walking the kids to school, working out and playing my guitar, hanging out with the kids after school. All these things helped a lot, and allowed me to see the way forward with greater clarity, and helped me realize that acting emotionally in this situation was not going to get me out the other side in one piece. For today, I stood on the tightrope, unswayed by the swirling winds.

 ©2015

Day 336- I walked into the office early, because I knew Klein always got in early. I was never really sure why he got in early because he didn't do any actual work. I suspected it was a plausible excuse to leave his house early and escape his family.

This particular morning he was doing his usual internet searching/stalking and showed me a picture he had found of Berg in a swimming pool on a toy inner-tube, doing his best to look like a fun, relaxed guy. It was a pretty lame pic to be sure, and certainly wouldn't be something that I would put online, let alone on my Facebook page. At the same time, the fact that Steve Klein came into work early to do stuff like this was a whole different level of weirdness.

"Look at this picture of Berg..what the fuck is the matter with him?" Klein said

"I don't know……that is pretty lame." I did the perfunctory agreement with this statement, but was really waiting for us to get to the point about what had happened the last time I was in the office.

"Alright Chris, do you want to talk here or go in the conference room?"

©2015

"Let's go in the conference room, I don't need everybody overhearing us as they come into work in the morning."

We stepped back into the conference room that gave us great views of the harbor, where I often found my mind wandering during many previous "fake" meetings when Berg and Klein had battled it out over various nothings large and small.

We sat down, and I could tell I was calm. Of course, Klein had reasserted his whole "I don't give a shit I'm cool as a cucumber" demeanor, so I supposed this was going to go quickly.

"So...what happened? Why did you walk out the other day? I mean, I think I know, and I tried to call and talk to you, but in your text messages you said you weren't ready to talk."

"Steve, I was just upset about being called into HR. They basically wanted me to be their snitch about what is going on between you and Berg. They said they thought I was the most neutral person because I wasn't in the middle of it, Omar is having serious job performance issues and Jim is perceived as your right hand man."

Klein leaned back, trying to look relaxed again.

 ©2015

"And what did you tell them?"

"Basically nothing. I was in and out of there in less than five minutes. They asked me about what was going on and who was instigating the issues. I claimed to know nothing but that I had seen you two in meetings, but I had no idea what was said because I wasn't in the meetings."

"And that's it, you didnt' say anything else?"

"Nope, not really. However I can tell you this, they are coming after you. The questions she asked me were all coming from the perspective that you might be causing the issues with Berg, not the other way around. She was basically looking to me to confirm those suspicions and fill in the details"

"Yeah well...... they will find out what will happen if the try and fuck with me. I know a lot of people in this town, including one of the best employment attorneys in New York City....he gets paid over 700 dollars per hour, and if they try to fire me then I will take this place down...I swear to God."

He was getting animated now. The fact was that he had already been trying to "take this place down" for almost a year seemed to be totally lost on him. That he quoted how much his so-called

204   ©2015

attorney got paid per hour seemed like a curious statement that only pointed to his impotent weakness. Of course, I said none of this to him directly.

"Alright, well anyway, very little was said."

"Ok and you're not mad at me?" Klein let slip out.

I found this to be a curious question, as if a wounded little boy had temporarily just crept into his mind and asked this question.

"No it's cool. I just want to get back to work"

And with that, the meeting ended with a couple of jokes and me doing my best impression of Berg, something that always got Steve to crack a smile.

Day 365- Over the course of the last year, we had all periodically been going to trade shows around the country in effort to sell more and boost our relationships. Jim had started the trend successfully, and I had picked it up with some success in the hospitality industry. Omar and I had also gone to some shows as well in Las Vegas.

The only person who hadn't gone anywhere was Mitch Berg. As a person who was probably voted

©2015

"most rigid" in high school, traveling to unfamiliar places without it being planned out for him was not his forte. In order to travel, we had to get a show, make a business case for it and pitch it to both Steve and Andrew. Fortunately, Roberta didn't have a role in these decisions and generally showed no desire to.

Because it always had to be approved, Berg never wanted to take the risk of going to a show, dealing with all the uncertainty, and then coming back with no business. So he had basically ignored going to trade shows for the most part, choosing his preferred method of endlessly pounding bad cold calls, except when he finally realized he was missing out by not going to them. The few times he belatedly pitched a few trade shows to Klein, the results were predictably shot down.

However, because many of these shows had been successful from a business perspective, several were now booked in advance. Andrew had decreed that everyone should have an equal chance to go to a show, because this way nobody could say that favoritism was at work. This meant that Berg would go to one, and that somebody would have to go with him because nobody could go to a show alone, and that was a fact that was doubly true

206

for Mitch. Somebody had to make sure he didn't go off the rails in front of prospects and clients.

This was the scene that was set today when Klein called me to his cubicle, where he, myself and Azov all adjourned to a conference room with the door closed.

"So, Andrew has decided that everyone, even Berg, should get the opportunity to go to one of the trade shows we have scheduled in the upcoming months." Klein said.

Azov and I both looked at each and smiled and rolled our eyes.

"I know nobody really wants to go with Berg, but the reality is, one of you guys will have to. There is no way I'm sending Omar to a show with Mitch....that would be a total disaster, plus Omar already went to a show with you Chris, so that leaves the show in Myrtle beach as the one that Berg is going to. So.......ah....it really comes down to which one of you wants to go with Berg....." Klein offered.

We were both silent for a minute, then Azov spoke up.

 ©2015

"I mean, I don't want to go with him, but if Chris doesn't want to go then......I guess that I will...but it will be a nightmare." Jim said, carefully hedging his bets.

There was a brief silence and then I spoke up.

"Obviously, I don't want to travel and spend 7 hours in the trade show booth with Berg, but I would if I had to...I guess...." I said hesitantly.

More silence, as Azov and I basically tried to wait each other out.

"I mean, I guess I could go" Azov said weakly.

I briefly considered what was at stake. I knew that I was probably the best choice, which was a relative term, in handling Berg in this situation. He outwardly didn't affect me as much, and staying calm with him was a big part of keeping him in check.

That being said, it wasn't easy. However, I sort of wanted to check out Myrtle beach as well because I hadn't been there in a long time. Still.....it was going to be bad spending three days with Berg. He was always very needy and wanted to spend a lot of time together on the road, whether he actually liked you or not.

 ©2015

"Fine...I'll go...but I want you guys to know that I am taking one for the team here. I hope you both realize that!" I finally blurted out.

We all laughed and then went into our usual round of making fun of Berg for a few minutes in our imitation Berg voice, imagining all the obnoxious things he would do on the road.

Little did I know our imagination wasn't nearly vivid enough.

Day 380- After many tedious moments of scheming my reservation so I wouldn't have to sit next to Berg on the flight, the day for our trip to Myrtle beach arrived.

We were flying an ultra low budget airline because it was the only direct commercial flight. As such, every passenger on these types of airlines were subjected to a series of unending pitches and up-sells to spend more money above the dubiously named "base fare".

This sales onslaught filtered through Berg's highly rigid temperament and threw him into a tizzy as he tried to understand the minutiae of every up-sell offer he was receiving, from boarding first, to

 ©2015

paying for carry-on bags, to the byzantine rules of their frequent flier program.

Luckily, by not sitting next to him, I didn't have to listen to his anxiety filled chatter about all these various conundrums.

I met Berg at the gate, where he stood amongst a motley throng of bedraggled fliers who may have looked more at home on a cross country wagon train then on a modern airliner.

Undoubtedly, he was there very early in attempt to settle his anxiety about flying into the unknown, even though this was a trip that he had aggressively angled for once he knew it may be in the offing. He seemed like a guy who didn't really know what to do once he had gotten the prize, except to decide that there could be danger lurking around every corner. On top of this, he was acutely aware of my attempts to avoid him, without overtly saying so. I had a very strong suspicion that this was a recurring theme with most people in his life, but it still pissed him off. He had a real talent for bringing out the worst in everyone.

Eventually we boarded the plane and took off without incident, making the flight from NYC to

©2015

Myrtle Beach in a couple of hours. I sat in sweet silence, with Berg more than 15 rows ahead of me. I was thankful that I couldn't hear the drone of his voice, as I was almost sure that he was verbalizing non stop to some poor soul that drew the short straw and had to sit next to him. For Berg, it seemed that talking gave temporary relief to the unending anxiety of his inner demons, and the bizarre and often unhinged world that they inhabited.

After landing, I met him at the gate and we had our usual tensely awkward exchanges about the mundane process of getting one's luggage and getting a cab. As was his practice, it was much more complicated than it needed to be.

Once we got in the cab, he began regaling myself and the cab driver about the woman he was chatting up on the airplane, her life history, her status (divorced and single), her kids. As mostly a way to entertain myself I pitched a softball comment to him, one I already knew the response to.

"Maybe you should've gotten her number Mitch…" I said.

  ©2015

"Actually, I did. She gave it to me no problem." The pride and ego in his voice immediately evident, always curiously positioned next to his crushing insecurity and child-like wanting.

"Thats great...maybe you should give her a call." I offered up

"No, I would never do that, I have had a SERIOUS girlfriend for over 4 years..."

The fact that he said this, even though he had already shared that fact with me countless times in the past, made no difference. It seemed the declaration was mostly for his own internal reassurance, as I'm pretty sure the cab driver didn't care at all because he hadn't said a word since Berg's verbal gusher had begun.

We arrived at our hotel, a reasonably nice place situated right on the beach, and went to our rooms. As I left to go to the elevator, it appeared Berg was having some predictably minor confrontation with the front desk about something, but I didn't stick around to find out.

He had already made sure in the cab to get me 'on the schedule' for that evening to have dinner together. While I didn't want to do this, I was trying to overcome my selfish impulses and

212   ©2015

decided I would give it a try, even though many previous experiences with him gave me a pretty good indication of how the evening was going to go. Who knows, he may even expense the dinner and try and charge me for half like he did last time!

For my own part, I had travelled alone extensively for business in previous jobs, and it didn't bother me in the least...I would've preferred to be left to my own devices than have to endure several more hours of Mitch Berg that were marinated in alcohol and food that he would wolf down and then immediately complain how it wasn't up to his standards. Then he would tell me he ate like this because he was "a growing boy." Ugh.

As evening approached, I met Mitch at the appointed time and we decided to walk to dinner. Meanwhile, I had checked my email up in my room and had already received four emails and two texts from Steve telling me not to be nice to Berg while he simultaneously pressed me for information on what Berg was doing, and speculating on what a jerk he might have been.

Between the two of them, I wished I could somehow teleport myself to a different universe.

©2015

Day 381- Our purpose in being in Myrtle beach was to occupy a booth at trade show and attempt to sign deals. Going into a show like that, I always tried to generate some good "vibe' with whomever I was working with, and despite my general aversion to Berg, I tried to put that aside for a few moments and do the same today, as it could only serve to help the cause.

"Let's have a good show today and see if we can sign some deals" I then stuck out my hand for a handshake....a sort of pep talk gesture before we stepped onto the 'playing field'

Berg was quick to make his statement.

"I'm always working to sign deals, always will be..." he then stuck out his hand and what ensued was what can only be described as the "power shake".

It is an attempt by the person shaking your hand to adjust their grip at which point they have the bones in your hand in an awkward position and then squeeze as hard as possible. It's intent is to assert dominance and cause pain to the other person if possible, and its patently obvious when someone tries to do it.

214   ©2015

Mostly it's a juvenile macho guy thing, but there had been one or two times as an adult that I remember other men doing it that I was meeting for the first time. At this point I had known Berg, at least superficially, for 8 years. I mostly remembered the 'power shake' from my High school days or when my brother used to give me a hard time as a kid.

I had a visceral reaction, mostly because I just felt like Berg's sole mission in life was to ruin any type of positive connection or normal moment he might have with another human being, even though on some level, that is what he desperately craved. He was utterly lost.

"What the fuck was that Mitch?" I snapped.

"What do you mean? I was just shaking your hand?!" Berg said, sounding incredulous.

"No you weren't you were doing that weird power move handshake thing.."

Of course the next response I should've seen coming from miles away.

"No I wasn't, what are you talking about? I just have a very firm grip." He said this with pride as if

 ©2015

he was letting his Daddy know that he was strong and had a firm grip.

I just shook my head and quickly realized that this was going to devolve into another pointless conflict that Berg would feel the need to pursue to its illogical conclusion. I therefore decided to say nothing and tried to address the matter at hand, which was to go to our booth and get situated and bring home some business.

Arguing with Berg was only going to make my purpose harder. But it took every ounce of determination to achieve this goal, as the rest of the day would soon show.

Meanwhile, my phone was blowing up with text messages from Klein, Azov, and Ahmedy who were dying to get the play by play of Bergs antics. Berg seemed to sense this, as he has a PHD in paranoia, and even a broken clock is right twice a day, or something like that.

Despite the fact he steadfastly and proudly refused to get a smartphone, he was working hard to look at mine and steal glances to see who was texting me. I had to turn off the volume and make sure whenever the phone was out of my hands it was placed on the table facing down.

  ©2015

"Wow, you just got another text huh?" he would occasionally say.

"Who was it? Who texted you?...was it the office?..whats going on there?"

"My family.....Yep, I'll be right back" I knew this response would drive him nuts, but at the same time it was necessary because he would literally look over my shoulder as I was typing while pretending to do something else. He had no qualms about that and seemed almost obsessively compelled to lurk around the booth.

Once the show began and potential clients began walking through, the strange power moves by Berg only got worse.

From a business perspective, I was pretty much set before I ever went on this trip. In other words, I didn't need it, but I was going to take my shots with potential clients as they presented themselves. Berg, on the other hand, was operating with his customary desperation and was behind the 8 ball on his numbers for the month. Consequently, he needed this show, and he acted as though his life depended on it. This was usually when he did his worst work, as people could smell

217   ©2015

his desperation and rapid high pitched nasal NYC speech pattern a mile away.

It never occurred to Berg that he was in the South, and adjusting your approach may be a good idea. You didn't want to come off like the stereotypical NYC character that these people had seen on TV their whole lives if you wanted them to connect with you and do business. In the early years, I used to try and tell him this in a nice way, but I learned rather quickly that he took instruction as an affront and insult. Regardless, he had long ago earned the title in my mind as "untrainable".

Adjustments were not part of his playbook, and as people walked by the booth, he would assume a stance in the middle of the booth, arms spread wide on the table in front of him in the "sales space" so he could somehow take up as much territory as possible in what seemed like a bizarrely awkward attempt to marginalize my presence. Apparently he thought he could grab "dibs" on any potential client who walked by, not thinking of how this strange stance might have looked to a passerby.

It was both comical and pathetic, because Berg had no idea how ridiculous he looked, especially to people who didn't know him. However, he had

 ©2015

no problem conducting a virtual verbal assault on anybody who came near the booth, whether they were signaling interest or not, and whether they were qualified for our offering or not. Such signals were outside the scope of Berg's awareness.

To him, it didn't matter, he was going to get his ineffective pitches out, he was going to collect his business cards, and he was going to put contracts in front of people who had no interest in signing them. Then his speech would grow increasingly rapid, unceasing and nonsensical while his tone would become more high pitched and shrill as he sensed people backing away from his uncomfortably close proximity to their personal space.

The poor devil was a prisoner of himself it seemed, completely unable to figure out why. But any sympathy I met've felt for him was balanced by the fact I knew he would throw me under the bus at any moment if he perceived there might be an advantage to him doing so. And his perceptions at any given time were rarely rooted in type of objective reality.

It reminded my of my Red Cross lifesaving training when I was teenager...something about how a

 ©2015

drowning person will drown their rescuers in an attempt to save themselves and stay above water.

Most of the 6 hours that we were in the booth together was spent with me listening to Berg to make sure he didn't say something that was patently false in an attempt to induce people to sign sales agreements so he could bring a positive report back to Klein. Klein was putting him under intense pressure to make numbers, even though Klein didn't really care about that, but it was a good excuse to harass Berg for a "legitimate" reason that wouldn't get him a further write-up to HR.

By the end of the show, I was psychologically exhausted just dealing with him. He was like a slow motion train wreck, and countering him or just watching to make sure he didn't do something that put the department into a precarious legal position was exhausting. I had more than enough of him, and just needed to go back to my room and get some "alone" time and maybe go out to a decent dinner....by myself.

However, Berg hadn't had enough of me...he wanted to spend the whole evening together. I knew it wasn't because he liked me per se...I'm not really sure anyone with that much self

  ©2015

loathing liked anyone all that much...but more it was a way to quiet the storm of internal anxiety with a lot of extroverted alcohol fueled jibber jabber nonsense. As for myself...I only wanted peace.

As we walked out of the convention hall after the show, Berg noticed there was an old-school shoe shine stand set up in the lobby. Apparently this triggered some type of nostalgic sub-routine in his head because he immediately reacted.

"Heeeey check it out, there is a shoe shine guy! I really need to get my shoes shined and 5 bucks is a lot cheaper than in New York, lets go get our shoes shined!" he said with glee.

From my perspective, I had reached my limit....if I had to be with him one more minute without a break, I was going to snap and go off on him. I knew that when I did that, it could get ugly very quickly.

"No, I'm going to head back to the hotel." I said, quiet but determined.

"C'mon it'll be fun...." Berg said, doing his best to sound jocular and charming in a human sort of way.

221   ©2015

I was adamant, this wasn't happening for me, and I was building up frustration at an alarming rate.

"Nope, heading back to the hotel, I'll see you later for dinner." I gave him dinner as a consolation prize to separate from him now...I had to, before I did something I'd regret.

"C'mon, just hang out for a minute it will only take two seconds."

Nothing ever took two seconds, especially when it concerned Mitch Berg.

"Nope, I'll see you later" I stated firmly.

I strode quickly for the exit, thrilled with the prospect of not having him next to me. As the door opened I saw the fading light of the late spring sun from the windows. I heard Berg admonishing me from behind as the door closed on him. I was free at last to breathe in the fresh sea air...and alone... blissfully alone for the next several hours.

I returned to my room at the hotel, watching the sun set over the Atlantic and I killed time for several hours watching a marathon of Amish Mafia while answering a lot of very funny texts from Omar and Jim, as well as a call from Steve.

   ©2015

Needless to say, Klein was much more interested in what Berg was doing and any potential dirt he could dig than how business was going at the show. The fact that I had to correct Berg while he was talking to a potential client from completely misrepresenting himself I left unsaid with Klein. It would've ignited a whole firestorm that I wasn't prepared to listen to and it would've served no purpose.

As I knew he would, at 5:30p sharp Berg called my room to get his evening meal plans all lined up. The idea of taking a night off and ordering room service was anathema to him, and if you didn't meet up with him in the evening he would be very offended. Somewhere in his book of rules that only he knew about, you met up with anyone you were on business with for breakfast and for dinner each night. I'm guessing he wrote that "rule" for himself on his first business trip in 1984.

I had already bucked this trend by not meeting for breakfast, as I had rightly predicted it would be a very long day in the trade show booth with him. He was a little like radon...you had to limit your daily exposure for health reasons.

I met him in the lobby of the hotel at 7pm and we stepped out onto the street to assess our dinner

 ©2015

options. Anytime a meal was involved, especially in a non-New York City locale, Berg had a lot of talking to do. A self-described "foodie", he was the resident expert on all things food, and never grew tired of simultaneously talking about and condescending a given areas food options.

At this stage of the game, I knew better than to really say anything, as the more I said, the more he would double his speech output to overpower me with a tsunami of words. The best I could hope for was to just yes him to death while he prattled on, and try and drink my way through it until it was over.

We settled on some fish place, and Berg of course had his usual 50 questions about obnoxious details for the waiter, who clearly wasn't a metro-sexual from Chelsea in NYC.

"Is your Chilean sea bass sourced from US or South American purveyors?" he said to the waiter.

"I'm not really sure but I can check for you...."

"You know something, thats ok. Also, do you sauté that or grill it?" Berg asked in rapid succession.

"Um, I think the menu...yes...right here....it says grilled Chilean Sea bass." the waiter said.

 ©2015

"Oh.....Ahhhh...Oooooh yeah....exactly, but I still just wanted to check and make sure. Is there any way you can sauté that?"

"Um, I think so, but I'd have to check with chef."

"Ok, please do that...and if it is sautéed, what type of oil do you use...is it olive oil, corn oil...what exactly is it?"

"I really am not sure sir. I have to see if we can do that I will get back to you."

"Ok great, let me know...oh yes and by the way, can we get some multi-grain rolls for the table?" Berg asked insistently.

"I can get you some bread sir, but I'm sorry its not multi-grain."

"Reeaally?... Woooow...hard to believe! What kind of rolls are they? Do you have any baguettes?

"Do we have any what?" the young waiter asked, confused by the rapid fire interrogation.

"Baguette's, you know French bread?" Berg said with a perturbed and abrasive tone to his voice.

"No, I think we just have regular rolls...." the waiter said weakly.

   ©2015

"'Regular' rolls? (throat clear) What does that mean? Are they whole wheat? or multi-grain? I'm really trying to watch my white flour intake. My doctor says its a good idea to watch my glycemic index. Plus, I'm a growing boy!"

"I'll check for you..."

"No..No...tell you what skip the bread and just bring me an appetizer plate of steamed kale and garlic."

"Sir, I don't have steamed Kale, I can bring you a house salad or sautéed spinach if you'd like.."

It went on like this for another 2-3 minutes, as Berg played his little food snob game of "stump the waiter from a small town" and silently took satisfaction making him dance.

I finally got to put my order in 5 minutes later, and ordered a stiff drink to take the edge off of this asinine display, as I knew that I had a lot of "listening" left to do before this train wreck of an evening drew to a close. Luckily, I found it much easier when I wasn't sober. While this may not have been good for my health, it helped my sanity greatly.

  ©2015

We finished dinner and ambled back toward the hotel. We stopped into the bar that was directly next door, the kind of semi-dive beach place that populated towns like Myrtle Beach all over the coastlines of America. There was something comforting about it.

It apparently was one of the last bars that still allowed smoking inside, and the early season golfers were in there with their big bellies, khakis and too tight polo shirts, along with a few of the local ne'r do wells mixed in. I saw the Karaoke stand as an opportunity for me to take leave of Berg for a few minutes.

I got up in front of packed house and did the Doors "Break on Through". Few in the crowd seemed to notice as every other song I had heard previously that night was country & western. As I returned to Berg, he seemed visibly depressed or angry, I couldn't tell which. I don't think verbal silence suited him much however. He made some annoying negatory comment about the Doors as we finished our drinks and made for the exit.

We parted ways that evening, agreeing to meet the next morning before heading over to the convention hall. Little did I know that the

 ©2015

strangest part of my trip with Berg had not even begun.

Day 383 - After another annoying day at the trade show yesterday, it was finally time to end this trip and go home. Berg chose to punish himself with the idea that he was going to fly back to the office on a Friday morning early and go into the office from the airport to "get a few hours of calls in" that Friday afternoon. He loved to tell everyone that late Friday afternoon was one of the best times to reach people, probably because it was the exact opposite of everyone else's experience.

The concept of old school "logging hours" and "doing time" was always an important one for him. He paid far less attention to whether those hours were effective or if he was meeting his numbers. To be in his cubicle, spinning his wheels daily and being tortured by his boss...this seemed to be what he wanted as much as possible. The reality of the matter was that nobody even cared if he came into the office on a travel day, not even Klein. There were 17,000 employees at our company, and nobody was watching him that closely.

 ©2015

He was on the 8a flight and I opted for the noon flight, both on Spirit air. Meanwhile, a severe "Noreaster" early spring storm had moved into the NYC area.

As it turned out, Berg's flight was delayed.

While this information was available online to anyone who bothered to use a computer, Berg chose to go to the airport and wait it out. We had been in touch more than I would've liked as he gave me the play by play updates of delays that kept pushing back his departure time as the weather had completely socked in Laguardia in NYC. I am sure the level of uncertainty was making him a basket case.

He had called the office and seemed to deliberately set himself up for a drubbing by Klein, who could sense Berg's mounting anxiety and sought to make it worse by putting more pressure on him to get home quickly, even though he knew it was totally unnecessary and that it was weather related beyond his control. Knowing Klein, he probably wanted to force Berg to get back early, and then leave the office early himself just so Berg wouldn't be able to be seen and "checked in" by him. Then Klein would harass him about it on Monday.

 ©2015

Berg was calling me every hour with updates, which I immediately pushed to voicemail, because I was due to leave from the same airport at Noon. I knew where this was going...he wanted to meet at the airport if my flight got delayed.

After two days of doing time with him....I just...I just couldn't fathom having to spend another moment in his company. Finally, the flight was cancelled and Berg got grudging permission from Klein to go back to the hotel and stay another day as there was no room on my flight, which would likely be delayed as well.

For my own part, I was keeping tabs on my flight online, but I eventually went to the airport to see if I could get on. It turned out the flight was continually being delayed for the two hours I was there...and then finally, around 6p was cancelled.

As a veteran flier, I saw this coming and had managed to book myself on a flight out the following day, betting that my original flight would be cancelled. Many people at the gate were not so lucky, as they had blindly listened to the gate agents telling them todays flight would take off eventually, even though it was cancelled in the end.

  ©2015

Meanwhile, while I was at the airport, I was getting nonstop texts and calls from Berg, who was back in his room at the hotel and apparently climbing the walls with anxiety and uncertainty. Never mind the fact he had a beautiful ocean front view and loads of time to enjoy it, he wanted to spend his time calling and texting me so he could lock me up for the evening meal if my flight did eventually get cancelled.

At this point, I was getting more than a little intimidated and freaked out, as my own family didn't call me nearly as much as Berg had in the last 6 hours. Moreover, each time he called, the voicemail sounded like the pathetic cold calls he made in the office, as if I hadn't known him for the last 8 years. By the time I finally knew I wasn't departing today, I wasn't going to let Berg know, and did I not respond to his calls as I hopped into cab to go back to the hotel. I had no interest in spending more quality time with him, and felt that I might get really nasty towards him if I did.

Stepping out of the cab back at the hotel, I became keenly aware, almost paranoid, that Berg was hunting me and could be lurking anywhere...in the lobby, out on the street. I half expected him

 ©2015

to jump out of the bushes in a camouflage suit. It was a very strange and unsettling feeling.

I re-checked into a different room, half expecting to see Berg on the elevator when the doors open.

Luckily he wasn't.

As I settled in, I tried to comfort myself with the thought that Berg had no idea if I had gotten on the plane, and therefore didn't know that I was back at the same hotel he was. I had no car in the garage, so there really was no way he could know I was here.

I was getting texts from Omar and Azov, and our hilarious back and forth banter regarding the office, Klein and Berg was a welcome diversion. After about an hour, I got another call from Berg, which I promptly sent to voicemail. I changed my clothes and tried to relax watching TV. I listened to the voicemail, against my better judgement, on a whim.

"Hello Chris, this is Mitch Berg calling you. I am now back at the hotel because my flight got delayed. I got permission from Steve to stay an extra day, so I don't know if you are coming back here, but if you are, we should definitely have dinner tonight. Give me a call at ...."

 ©2015

He then went on to recite as number twice, even though he knew I had it in my phone for the last 5 years. The voicemail made my skin crawl, as he used his same officious cold call voice that he always used, and I dreaded the message before I even listened to it.

As I sat there, the room "landline" phone rang. This scared the shit out of me because in recent years, it is very rare for a hotel room phone to ring at all, and if it did, it couldn't be good. Everyone has cell phones and everyone knows that the room phone costs a fortune to use, unless you were calling room to room within the same hotel.

I knew immediately who it was. It had to be Berg. I called down to the front desk to make sure that they had not called me for any reason and they assured me that they hadn't. I let the first call ring out without picking up, and then it immediately began ringing again.

And then it rang again a third and fourth time.

This was stalking scary....because this meant that Berg had somehow managed to bamboozle the front desk into revealing I was checked in, and what my room number was. I knew him well enough to know this is certainly something he

 ©2015

would have no shame in doing. I didn't answer these calls either, but I was truly freaked out that he would go this far just to have someone to hang out with. I reminded myself that taking a hint was not in his playbook, as if I hadn't already learned this lesson a thousand times before.

My mind was racing as to what my next move was, as I was positive that he was going to knock on my door at any minute and ask to go to dinner, then browbeat me for giving him the dodge. I decided to order pizza to the room and worriedly began looking at the peep hole through the door, trying to watch the hallway to see if he was lurking. Berg had clearly gotten inside my head, and I hated it.

I turned off my cell phone, unable to face it if he were to call again, and suddenly feeling like a caged rat in my hotel room. After awhile, I decided I wanted some beers to take the edge off this feeling of psycho stalking that I was under.

Of course, that would require me to go out. By now it was dark, and at least I had the cover of darkness in my favor in making my way to the gas station that sold beer two blocks from the hotel.

I slipped out of my room, Rambo-like, looking around corners and down from the balcony below

©2015

to see if I could spot Berg. By now my head was seriously playing games with me as I was beginning to think he was some omnipresent force that knew what I was doing at any given moment.

At street level, I quickly ran across the street, trying to minimize my exposure to any potential lines of sight that he might have. I knew this was crazy, but the longer this went on, the more frightened and determined I was to not see him.

I had communicated some of this via text to Azov and Ahmedy, who were really having a field day with it. It was a lot funnier from a distance, but I also could see the humor in it...to a point.

I was lucky to make it back to my room without encountering Mitch, and spent the rest of the night holed up in my hotel room, waiting for the next day to come, and hoping that the phone didn't ring or that I didn't get a knock on my door.

©2015

Day 389- Flying out last week was more or less uneventful, and I arrived back home with no further encounters with Berg. As I sat at my desk catching up on work and inputting new deals, I was getting nonstop text and chat's from Ahmedy, Azov and Klein, wanting to joke and dish on all the various shenanigans with Berg while on the trip. If they didn't have the courage or stupidity to hang out with Berg on a trip, they certainly were going to get all the vicarious details of the bizarre experience.

After at least an hour of this silence, Berg ambled over to my cube, anxious to make his comments. I knew this moment was coming, and I dreaded it. He was going to force a confrontation about how I avoided him, or at the very least bring it up and then talk around it.

"So did your flight get out on Saturday?" he pretended to ask innocently, knowing full well that it did not, but wanting to see if I would lie to him.

"Nope, I ended up sticking around the airport and it eventually got cancelled so I went back to the hotel, let Steve know I was staying an extra day due to flight cancellations, and checked back into a different room."

   ©2015

The wooden smile flashed across his face, reminding me of Richard Nixon.

"Reeeaally? Woooow..so you and I were at the same hotel again Friday night! You should've called me and we could've had dinner. I tried to text you but got nothing back...I figured you were on the plane." he stated..showcasing his acute lack of convincing acting skills.

I had my stock excuse ready for this moment. It wasn't my first go-around with these types of interrogations from him.

"Yeah I was really tired and just decided to go back to the room and hang out before..."

Immediately, Berg cut me off.

"Really? Wow.... thats too bad..because I went out and had a really nice dinner that night at that place across the street that we looked at. I met some cool locals who were telling me about the history of Myrtle Beach and some of the stories of what it was like there years ago. My food was excellent as well, I had Chilean monkfish with artisanal cheese and raspberry sorbet for dessert. Did a couple of tasting shots of whiskey. Too bad you missed it. Food was pretty good considering

 ©2015

where I was at. Much better than the night we went out.... "

This statement would be funny as a perverse and pathetic lie if it weren't so utterly predictable. He got his chance to completely deflect his own crazy behavior that night with even more insane behavior now, putting me in the position of either ignoring what he did, or having to challenge him on it, which he would then vehemently deny and assert that I was paranoid or crazy. Luckily, I knew this.

"Cool." was my reply.

And this is what drove him more crazy than anything. Berg always enjoyed any type of attention he could get from people....he actually seemed to prefer the negative type mostly. What really made him crazy and drove him nuts was indifference or people ignoring him. And in his world, people were always ignoring him or not giving him the mountains of respect he felt he was entitled to. I viewed indifference as the only card I could play in trying to limit my interactions with him...and it worked like a charm. My only goal was to get him to walk away.

238   ©2015

Berg stood there at my desk, and I stared at my monitor, feeling his eyes burn holes in the side of my head and the thick tension of his barely suppressed fury permeating the air. I had to be steady, I said to myself, and show no emotion. I kept typing away on my keyboard, careful to block the text I was sending to Azov as Berg stared at me. It was all about being calm under pressure.

Finally Berg walked away, head bobbing from side to side with his unusual gait...in a huff because he was unable to get the conflict that he sought so desperately....and I was able to resume ignoring him as much as possible while the shit storm continued to swirl around me.

 ©2015

Day 400- I got in early today for some reason that I haven't quite yet figured out. Heading up the elevator, it occurred to me that, after over a year, we were due to start earning some commission off of the first deals that we signed back when I started.

This was also a big deal for Steve because it served as a sort of validation of his leadership that he was able to drive revenue for the division. He and Azov had been huddled in conference rooms quite a bit lately, apparently speaking to Andrew on calls and trying to get a complete handle on how much revenue was going to be brought in.

This had been going on for several weeks, off and on, and around 2:30p on this day we received an email from Klein stating that we were going out after work for drinks. Of course, he wasn't going to invite Berg, so we all had to do the secretive routine the whole day and made sure that we each left the building separately in stages.

As the day progressed, I could tell that Klein wasn't in the greatest frame of mind, even for him, but he wasn't telling anybody what the problem was.

©2015

At around 4:30, we began ambling out of the office and convened at the tavern at the end of the dock right outside the building. It had a great view of Manhattan across the river, and the drinks were fairly low priced for the first few hours.

As we settled in at the bar, one by one, we each got our drinks. Klein was sitting next to me on one side, with Azov on the other. As was the custom, Omar was the last to arrive, always being the chronically slow one. However, his addition was always welcome as he was the funniest amongst us, even in the face of what we had to put up with on a daily basis.

Initially the talk was mostly making fun of Berg, as it was the one common thing we had between us. However, by the the second drink, I noticed that Klein stopped talking, and it was just myself, Azov and Berg talking and joking about any crazy thing that popped into our heads.

However, each of us was keenly aware that Klein was very quiet, and appeared to be descending into some type of bad place. Finally, Ahmedy went outside for a smoke and Azov followed him, eager to get away from Klein, who needed him like a security blanket. I saw Klein alone and decided to make my move.

 ©2015

"Steve, what's going on, are you Ok?" He seemed like a dejected little boy, almost sad. A vulnerability had crept in under the hard boiled exterior we usually saw each day. For a minute, despite my better judgement, I found myself feeling sympathetic toward him.

"Yeah, I'm fine….." his voice trailed off.

"That doesn't sound very convincing…c'mon whats going on? We're supposed to be having a good time." I said

"We got the revenue numbers in today from the project last year. I told Andrew the division was going to book $1.5 million, and it turns out its only going to be $400,000. Not only that, Andrew told corporate that we were going to book the higher figure, and he almost shit his pants when I told him what the new number was."

Klein communicated this news as if he was talking about being diagnosed with imminently terminal cancer.

"So, what does that mean? Are they going to shut down the division?"

Klein was silent for a minute, perhaps intrigued by the seductive idea of compounding bad news and

    ©2015

making it sound worse. That mindset was very well travelled for him, as I had seen it countless times in his interactions with all of us.

"No, they aren't going to do that, but Andrew was pissed."

"What do you mean, was he yelling or something?"

"No, nothing like that, he just said that he was going to need to get a drink after work and that he had to tell Sharon that the revenue numbers were a lot lower than he originally projected."

At this point I was a little buzzed, but by no means drunk. Klein had only had one drink.

"You know what Steve, you made a mistake... doesn't sound like something that we can't fix when the other half of the settlement comes through. We have a lot of clients for that one too. Let me get you another drink."

"No thanks. I can't because of my medications. If I have too many drinks while I'm on them it won't be good"

"What do you mean?" This was a new piece of information for me, but I had a feeling I knew what he was going to say.

 ©2015

"I'm on a bunch of different psych meds. Ask Azov.....he saw me when we had breakfast on the road. 7 different anti-depressants. Thats what I fucking tell Berg...he should get on them too and maybe he wouldn't be such a freak."

This explained a lot, even though it wasn't entirely surprising. Essentially, it seemed like Klein was in some type of pill induced haze on most days, which actually filled in a lot of the blanks concerning his behavior. Whatever these drugs were, they weren't helping, and were probably hurting, his outlook.

"Wow...that's a lot. Do you think they help?" I knew my opinion regarding the answer to this question, but I was very curious to hear his interpretation of the effectiveness of his drug regimen.

"Yeah...absolutely. But thats why I can't drink......of course....right now, I can't say I'm really too confident about what's happening." Klein offered.

"C'mon man, its nothing to get so down about, we'll get a lot more revenue the next time around" I offered.

"I've thought about it you know." Klein said to me unsolicited

244 ©2015

"Thought about what?" I asked, genuinely confused as to what he meant by this.

I looked out the window toward Manhattan as dusk fell. The almost completed Trade center stood directly across the Hudson. Azov and Ahmedy were outside, Omar smoking a cigarette. I had brief feeling of frozen time, of this moment, of some type of eternity within it. It didn't make any sense, but most feelings like that didn't.

"About killing myself. I have it all thought out. I would line up all the pills, get a bottle of Jack and just do all of them at once and down as much Jack as I could."

I was a bit taken aback, as I wasn't ready for this sudden revelation of his darkest thoughts. This was a man with a wife and two teenage sons, who clearly was every bit as close to the edge as his favorite nemesis, Mitch Berg, ever was. I recovered quickly, trying to arrest his slide into the mental abyss. I may have thought Klein was a horrible boss, which he was, but on a human level I knew that he had a family that counted on him. I tried to remind myself that deep down, I was still a good guy....or at least I hoped I was.

©2015

"Steve, you have a wife and kids who would be very sad if you ever did that." I said.

"No they wouldn't. My son hates me. He told me once he thinks that I don't love him."

Somehow, this didn't surprise me at all. Steve didn't seem like the kind of guy who told anyone he loved them. He seemed more like the type that if he loved you, if he felt that vulnerability that is such a crucial part of true love, he was going to browbeat you even more just to deny it, mask it, or cover it up.

"I doubt that he hates you Steve, he is just a teenager and teenagers say a lot of things they don't mean." I said.

"My wife wouldn't care, she thinks I'm nuts."

While I continued to try and buck him up, I could totally see why his wife and kids may not appreciate his presence, for much the same reason I didn't. He really was just a pretty nasty, conniving guy on many levels. But what I learned in even greater detail on this day was that there was a wounded little boy underneath all that, very unsure of himself, and trying to be recognized and heard. At least thats how it seemed to me.

 ©2015

Soon, Azov and Ahmedy came back inside and sat at the bar, and the topic immediately switched back to Kleins' comfort zone, which was Berg bashing and vocal imitations. The moments of honesty from him had come and gone like a quick mouse scattering across the floor.... and now it had disappeared into a crack in the wall...not to be heard from again.

Azov ordered another round with shots, and as time went on, kept signaling to me how he was waiting for Klein to go home so he could relax and hang out. Clearly, his role as the "chosen one" by Klein was beginning to grate on him as he could never shake the guy. Klein literally counted on him to read the menu, figure the tips on a bill....Omar and I used to joke that Klein would probably ask him to go to the bathroom with him if he could get away with it.

Azov drank his shot, and I took one with him. Ahmedy was driving, so he just sipped his second beer. Azov had whispered to me that he wanted me to commit to staying and drinking with him until Klein left. I hadn't really ever seen Azov get pissed like this, but there was fire in his eyes.....

"I'm gonna fuckin stay here until that asshole leaves. I am NOT walking out with him." Azov said

 ©2015

as he took another swig. He apparently had reached his limit of playing along with Kleins' craziness, as least for tonight. He also knew that walking out with him committed him to a half hour PATH ride back across the Hudson, a prospect he clearly didn't relish.

Klein often treated Azov as some sort of best-buddy security blanket, and really did seem to be staying at the bar far longer than he wanted to just so he could walk out the door with him.

It was actually kind of funny if it weren't so messed up and strange...everybody, save for myself and Omar, was freaking out. The bottled tension of months of sniping, coupled with the revenue gaffe, had pushed Jim and Steve over the edge in different directions.

Azov was realizing that being Kleins personal "teachers pet" was a thankless task that may have very few positive outcomes for him.

Klein was having a fleeting moment of clarity when he connected his outrageous actions and managerial style to the depths of feelings he was having now. He sat silent at the bar, looking into the distance with unfocused eyes, not saying anything.

248   ©2015

Eventually, he got up and mumbled something about having to catch a train and asked Azov if he wanted to leave. Jim firmly replied "No", and with that, Klein said goodbye and walked out. I had a sense that he knew the minute he was gone that we were going to begin breaking bad on him. In this regard he was not mistaken at all.

"Did you see him??" Omar said.

"Yeah, looked like somebody shot his pet cat." I muttered.

"He's all depressed because his revenue projections to Andrew were more than twice what we actually brought in. Now he's in a total panic because Andrew was a little upset. I hate his entire approach, its just so lame. He was making a much bigger deal out of it than Andrew was." Jim said.

"Really? Seems like Andrew would be pissed..." Omar offered.

Jim continued.

"Well, he was, but not so much at Steve, more at the fact that he had already told his boss what he was expecting our division to bring in. He made some comment that it was ok but that he was

249   ©2015

'going to need to grab a drink' after work." Jim explained.

"Geeze, the way Klein was talking to me, he made it sound like they were about to close us down in a minute. He was sitting there telling me his suicide scenario. Isn't that some type of warning...when people have planned out in detail how they are going to kill themselves? It was pretty whacked out." I said.

"Dude are you serious?" Omar said. He seemed genuinely surprised at this revelation.

"Yep, while you guys were outside having a cigarette he told me that he had it all planned out...he was going to OD on his meds once he lined them all up, and then drink Jack Daniels. He said it would be painless and that he would just go to sleep." I explained.

"Jesus, that guy is out of his mind" Azov spat out, boozy and riled up from just being in Klein's presence outside of work. He clearly was on a roll.

"Man, I don't know what is up with that guy, both him and Berg are nuts. They're made for each other." Ahmedy offered.

  ©2015

We hung out at the bar for another hour or so before ambling off into the evening to make our way home. While the portion of the evening with Ahmedy and Azov was fun, the earlier portion where the spectre of Klein held sway over the proceedings was more than a little disturbing on several different levels.

Klein was every bit as internally volatile as I had assumed, and tonight he had essentially proved it. He had overreacted to what was, in essence, a very preventable business mistake if he bothered to pay attention to his work half as much as he paid attention to torturing Berg and the rest of his employees. He then, in a moment that could be described as either weakness or clarity, had shown me a window into his inner world, and it was a very sad and bleak place. Why it was so sad and bleak didn't, on the surface, seem to have an easy explanation.

Klein had grown up in a world of privilege, attended Ivy League schools, obtained a law degree, had plenty of money, a family and a wife... all the boxes were seemingly checked....and yet still...something haunted and drove him to his increasingly bizarre behavior. The fact that some doctor, or several doctors, had seen fit to

          ©2015

prescribe him at least 7 different psycho-active pharmaceuticals spoke to this deep pain and confusion. My guess is that somehow Steve had manipulated the system and was in fact abusing these drugs.

Regardless, he wasn't one to embrace self help or introspection. His fleeting and singular moment of lucid honesty passed very quickly, and I had no doubt....not one....that he was ready to get back to his usual antics very shortly.

Day 405 - The days became increasingly pressure filled since we were at the bar. Klein seemed to be going to a lot of closed door meetings, some with Azov in tow, others not. Meanwhile Berg was walking around in a more tension filled haze than usual, making his idiotic and semi-nonsensical comments to anyone who happened to get within 2 feet of his cubicle. He was, as always, desperate for any type of attention and his anxiety only fueled the pressure to new heights.

He and Klein rarely spoke, and when they did, it was usually Klein who was trying to turn the simplest interaction into some sort of conflict that would end up making Berg counter-attack. Then

  ©2015

the minute he did that and Berg walked away, Klein would make sure he documented the incident for the HR war that was going on between them.

Meanwhile, Ahmedy was showing up for "work" later and later, and would take long mid-day sojourns into parts unknown. All of this would've been fine if he had been cranking out the numbers. However, he was doing basically nothing, and making sure everybody knew he didn't give a shit what went on in our department anymore. His morale was in the cellar, and he wasn't making any effort to disguise that he thought the whole thing was BS. This played right into Klein's natural negativity, and Omar, who once was viewed as a pivotal pawn in Klein's attempt to drive Berg crazy, was now viewed by Klein as a liability that he could not trust.

The rot in the department was continuing unabated and I could not help the feeling that the issues were coming to a head. I was actually astonished that it had been allowed to go on this long. However, I don't think Andrew really knew what was going on until Roberta was brought in on-site to actually oversee the craziness.

 ©2015

Day 468- My second summer had arrived at Sharetech, and somehow, despite everything, my personal production had held up very well. I was determined, for my families sake, to not lose this job. The harder I felt the pressure of Klein's horrible management, the more determined I became. My two plus years out of the job market had hardened me beyond belief, a fact that was both expected and surprising.

Somehow, I had managed to not get sucked down into the negative vortex that Berg, Klein and Ahmedy had been ensnared in. Jim was also having his issues with the increasing pressure that Klein was putting on him as the "teachers pet", but he was smart enough to keep his numbers up even while this was occurring. It almost seemed that 'real business' was a welcome respite for him from the daily grind of Klein and his constant need for Jim's attention on every single detail. He knew that management also saw this dynamic at work as well, because whenever there was an HR meeting, Klein liked to compare Berg's performance unfavorably to Azov's, putting Azov in the position as an accomplice to Klein's machinations.

While Azov was a much better salesperson, and "people person" in general, it was still an unfair

 ©2015

comparison in many ways because Klein had rigged the entire system of the department as one large trap meant to capture Berg in its clutches and create "reportable" offenses to HR that would eventually lead to him getting canned.

Today, Azov, Berg and myself had arrived at the usual time. It was unusual in that Klein was not yet in and Jim seemed to have no idea as to his whereabouts. Klein kept a high level of personal contact with Azov, and always informed him of what he was doing with orders to tell us when he deemed it appropriate.

Klein's custom was to always get in early, often telling us repeatedly how he left his house shortly after 6a, as if logging 10 plus hours at the office each day and getting nothing done but personnel harassment was somehow a badge of pride.

By noon time, we were all starting to wonder if he was coming in at all. As we walked out the door that evening, Klein never had showed that day and was officially a "no call, no show" for the day.

Day 469- Klein was in at his usual time today and informed both myself and Azov that he was renegotiating his contract with the company for

 ©2015

more money. When I first heard this I almost laughed, but managed to hold it in.

"These fuckin cheapskates need to realize that I am completely underpaid. This is the cheapest company I've ever worked for in 25 years." Klein spouted.

The fact that he was making over double what anybody else in the division was never occurred to him.

"And if they try to fuck with me, my sister in-law has contacts with the best employment law attorney in the city. I'll fuckin sue them for every last penny I deserve!"

Even for Klein this was an unusual amount of bluster and chest-thumping. He later revealed that he had been in the New York office the previous day for "contract negotiations".

I struggled to understand how any company would consider giving Klein a raise at all, and what was wrong with the world that this guy could get paid so much to create misery and simultaneously try to destroy business opportunities. He was always a complete and total liability on sales conference calls, and Jim and I had learned early on it was better to do these types of calls without him.

 ©2015

Klein prattled on about how bad the company was, how the people he was negotiating with in New York were idiots and tight-ass cheapskates, and how they had lied to him. For good measure, he threw in his usual trope about how the whole company hated our division.

I closed the day in a fairly demoralized state.

I couldn't help thinking that no matter what I did, no matter how hard I worked, that no good deed would ever go unpunished...that no matter what... corrupt systems would prevail, and the willfulness and determination that bad people have would always dominate over the cowardice and apathy that were evident in any attempts to stop them.

I feared for my family in such a world. Perhaps I had duped my children by bringing them here. It was my job to maintain optimism, as well as a steady income, in the face of this onslaught which felt more insurmountable with each passing day.

All I knew how to do was to hold it inside, go home, and make sure I showed up again the next day for whatever might await my fate.

It may not be a great option, but it was the only one I had.

      ©2015

Day 475- At 2p today, Azov and I were emailed by Andrew for an immediate call in one of the conference rooms. As luck would have it for both of us, Berg took an extremely rare day off.

At the appointed time we both went to the small conference room and dialed in. Andrew promptly came on the line in his thick English accent.

"Good day, is this Jim and Chris?" Andrew said in his forced 'upbeat' tone.

We both replied "Yes Andrew we're here"

"Magic....great" his tone was even. He continued.

"Is Omar there?"

Jim and I both looked at each other awkwardly. The truth of the matter was Omar wasn't with us and we had no idea where he was.

"No Andrew, he isn't here." It was all we could say without lying or making Omar look worse than he already did.

"Where is he?"

"Ahh, I don't know Andrew, do you know Chris?" Jim said to me.

 ©2015

"I have no idea Jim." I said, feeling sheepish but not knowing what else to say.

"Okay, that's a separate issue….Anyways, I wanted to let both of you know that Steve Klein no longer works with Sharetech and we have decided to move on."

There was a short, but noticeable pause before he continued.

"I can't really go into any specifics about that other than to say we thought it was best that he do so. Do you have any questions?""

We both looked at each other knowingly, our mouths open…but said nothing except….

"No Andrew, I don't think so, at least not right now."

Both Jim and I had been around long enough to know that at a big company with public market exposure, even if we did have questions, Andrew was not allowed to tell us anything without exposing many in the company to legal liability.

Andrew continued.

"So I'm going to be counting on your good selves and Mitch to help kind of get things together and

 ©2015

keep things running. The department isn't going anywhere, and I hope that this will be a positive step. In terms of countersigning the deals that come in, I want you to send them directly to me, I will get them countersigned and back to you in fairly short order."

Andrew continued on.

"Jim, I want you to go through Steve's desk and see if there are any pending deals in there that we need to look at more closely or anything that might be of importance. Chris, feel free to help him as needed. You guys have done a good job for us and I'm going to be counting on you until we figure out the next steps. As far as I'm concerned you are both more than capable of handling this and keeping things together in the interim."

I felt my spirits rising in utter relief in the fact that Klein wouldn't be back. I half expected a bright ray of sunshine from above to come down from the ceiling in our windowless conference room.

"I know that Mitch Berg is on a PTO today so I will address this with him separately when he gets back. Please don't say anything to him until I

©2015

speak to him as that is the proper protocol as far as HR is concerned."

There was silence for a moment and then....

"Do you have any questions?"

We both looked at each other and smiled.

"Not right now Andrew, thanks"

And with that, the call was over.

We sat back and just looked at each other. I personally was amazed at our good fortune. I think that Jim was happy, but also a little stunned as he had a much more ambiguous relationship with Klein than I did. I immediately started smiling, and so did Jim.

We had been delivered from the jaws of defeat, and we wouldn't have to worry about Steve Klein manipulating our lives any more.

Day 478- Jim, myself, and Berg watched this afternoon as Omar got out a box and packed up the considerable amount of bric a brac he had accumulated in the last year and a half around his cubicle. He had been fired about a half hour

 ©2015

before and seemed sanguine about his prospects. He knew this day had been coming for awhile... many days he seemed as though he was inviting it.

"Dude, I want to wish you good luck, but this place is going down. They aren't going to keep this division open, not with all the crap that has gone on here." He said to me.

I personally was willing to gamble otherwise, but I didn't bother to oppose his statement. There was no point to it.

"Yeah, well I hope that isn't true, but you never know. It's tough everywhere." I offered.

We all walked Omar downstairs to the lobby with his box. I was sad to see him go, as we had had many good times together. While he may not have been a great employee for Sharetech, I considered him a true friend who would give you the shirt off his back if you asked him to. He was also always a good guy to have "in the clubhouse" and knew how to lighten the mood when the situation called for it.

Even more out of sorts, of course, was Berg. He and Omar never got along, and he viewed Omar as "Jim's guy" because Jim had referred him and Steve had hired Omar over Berg's advice not to.

©2015

Even so, anything that was a change always threw Berg for a loop, and he did a hell of a job of acting shocked that this had happened.

It wasn't particularly surprising to anybody else, but Berg just kept going on and on about how he couldn't believe it.

We said goodbye to Omar as he walked out the revolving door. He gave us a couple of winks when he knew Berg wasn't looking. That was for all the "Berg voice" imitations we had done in the past. Jim and I smiled knowingly.

And with that the department was down to 3.

In the coming weeks with Klein and Ahmedy gone, we all managed to pull together and get our house in order. What seemed so difficult when Klein was with us obstructing every activity was actually quite straightforward and easy with him gone. Things that had taken days or weeks took minutes or hours.

The president of our division came down for an obligatory lunch to pump us up, but it was fairly clear he didn't really understand what had gone on and didn't care to. Mostly he just seemed overworked and relieved that the "noise" in our department had abated with the terminations.

 ©2015

And just like that...the hurricane force storm that had been brewing for better part of two years ended. No more problems....no more craziness.....just a silent vacuum where nothing but trouble had been before.

Sure, Berg was still his annoying and selfish self, but Jim and I knew how to minimize that, rather than whip it into a frenzy. We had known Berg for a long time, and consequently, we knew how to handle his substantial idiosyncrasies. When we got frustrated with him, which was often, we shut our mouths and used our phones to text back and forth privately as a stress reliever, keeping the vocal sniping and potential conflicts to a relative minimum.

In time...we all moved on, and looked back on the turmoil of that time with amusement, confusion... and in our darker solitary moments...horror.

Day 582 - About 6 months after Klein and Ahmedy left, Azov decided to make a move and take his career in another direction. I was sad to see him go, much as I had been with Omar, but had long since accepted this as a fact of the working world. We had been through a lot together and often

 ©2015

relied on each other as the sole voice of reason in an increasingly insane situation.

Today I received a call from Klein, who I hadn't heard from except for a few short personal emails since they day he had left 8 months before.

"Hi Chris, its' Steve. How is everything going?"

He sounded like his familiar self, no different than when I had first met him.

"Doing good Steve, how are you?" We exchanged pleasantries, and then Steve got to the point.

"I'm well. Listen, I wanted to get in touch with you because a contact I have over at one of your competitors is looking for a good, seasoned person like yourself to help pump up the deal volume and I immediately thought of you."

My first thought was that this was some type of manipulation on Klein's part, or perhaps some new way to strike at Berg that hadn't occurred to me yet. Regardless, I played it completely straight.

"Thanks Steve, I appreciate you thinking of me. I'm not sure that I'm actually looking right now." I said

 ©2015

"Listen to me, those cheap fucks are never going to give you a raise and they aren't going to pay you. They are going to wait until you get everything in and then they are going to shut the whole division down and just collect. I'm telling you, I know those guys. I know those people and how they act."

One thing that you could say for Klein, his ire never wavered and his story was always consistent in its message.

"Steve, I really appreciate it, is there any way you can email me the information, I suppose it can't hurt to give them a call."

Steve knew I was overdue for a raise and that it was a pain point for me. Thus, he knew my vulnerability and was playing straight into that. However, he also had tipped his hand.

"Yes, I will definitely do that and make sure you let them know that I sent you. That place is going down and you definitely do not want to be there when it does." Klein said.

Later we ended the call and I waited to see what he would send over. While I appreciated him thinking of me, I couldn't help that think this was some type of gamesmanship that fit his overall

 ©2015

plan. What exactly that manipulation was I wasn't quite sure of.

Later that day, Andrew called me and let me know I was getting a 50% raise. His timing could not have been more ironic, and I silently chuckled to myself as I walked out the door that night on my way to the train.

So much for shutting down the department.

 ©2015

Post Script   3 months later

Three months later in March, Andrew called Berg long distance from California in a near state of panic regarding a letter that had been received from an attorney in class counsel that was being referred to the judge on a settlement case we were working.

Andrew was particularly panicked because if the judge on any case we were working got wind of the fact we were acting in an unprofessional or illegal manner, he could throw us off working the case permanently. Needless to say, such an outcome could cost the division hundreds of thousands, if not millions of dollars.

The contents of this letter are listed below:

"To Whom it May Concern:

My name is LaShawnda Wright and I am the office manager at Engle Plastic and Reconstructive surgery in Manhattan, New York City. I am writing in regard to several phone calls that I have received from a Mitch Berg concerning his desire to sign us up for a service that he is offering in connection to a settlement refund.

268   ©2015

These calls have been, to say the least, harassing, misleading and rude. He has told us on more than one occasion that we must use his service in order to get money that we are entitled to from a settlement. He further has harassed our office by calling multiple times, often within the same day and has used foul language and an angry tone.

I am requesting that you put a stop to this harassing behavior and that you make sure that Mr. Mitch Berg does not engage in this behavior with anybody else and that his firm be punished. My boss's name is Dr. Seth Engle and he is also not pleased with the constant negative calls coming from Mr. Berg and the firm he works for. He will be contacting his attorney shortly to pursue this to the fullest extent of the law.

We request that you pay the utmost attention to this matter.

Sincerely,

LaShawnda Wright
Office Manager,
Engle Plastic & Reconstructive Surgery
512 48th St. Suite 1405
New York, NY 60422"

©2015

It was, on first look, certainly cause for alarm for both our division and Berg. However, it only took a couple of quick checks with Dr. Engle to realize the entire letter was fake. He had no LaShawnda working for him and Berg had never called there.

Mitch and I, upon learning this news, looked at each other.

The letter was very soon declared a fake by the court and ordered under seal. It ended up being a complete non-issue that caused a brief panic for about 2 hours one Friday afternoon. I think Berg probably wanted to change his shirt after the long distance interrogation that Andrew had given him before he knew it was a fake.

However, despite the fact it was essentially unprovable, both Berg and I knew who wrote the bogus letter.......

It was Steve Klein for sure.

Now it became very clear to me what Klein had in mind for our division. He wanted to shut the division down, and this is why he had called me regarding the job a few months ago. In essence, it was part of his plan to remove the last solid producer from the department while simultaneously taking out Berg with the phony

270   ©2015

smear letter that he had sent. It appeared that he had been plotting this "take down" attempt since he had left, presumably as his last act of vengeance against the company and Berg. The fact that it was rather transparent and clumsily executed was besides the point.

Pathetic, but all the pieces fit together.

Since that phone call, and after the phony letter, I had not heard anything from Klein at all.

His LinkedIn page posted a vague blurb about him working somewhere in the city...but where exactly he was lurking, spending his days, we never did find out. It wasn't a stretch to say that Berg was looking over his shoulder for months afterward, and it was also true that I also found myself thinking about whatever Klein may have in store for us next as he sought to make good on his threat to "take this department down". However, so far, he had not succeeded and if I have my way, he never, ever will.

None of us escaped from our time with Steve unscathed, and to say that there were no true winners, only survivors seems painfully accurate. We had all gone down a dark path, created by the economic ruin of the times, the associated clash

©2015

of personalities, and the dark shadows that lurked within each one of us, waiting to be drawn out and given voice in the face of uncertainty. The utter pointlessness of the all that had occurred during those two years could not be escaped and often left me wondering where such storms came from and where they went when they eventually blew away, leaving an inevitable crush of destruction in their path.

THE END

©2015

And for me, revenge and destruction was it's own reason, it's own purpose and it's own reward. I didn't need to answer to anyone but myself, and I had done that in spades. They couldn't stop me, so they joined his side because he had threatened them. That's fine with me. They may have sided with Berg but I wasn't going to give them the satisfaction of letting them know what I would do next. They will find out soon enough.

I had stood by my principles, and I hadn't backed down. In time they would know this, and know it well. In the meantime I can take solace in the fact that I had made his life miserable, that I had laid my burden down on him, the one who really deserved it more than I ever did. He was much worse than I ever was, and ever would be. Even my Dad would've seen that....even he would have agreed with me. Berg was a disloyal backstabbing bastard, and I never once bent to his will. I somehow believe, must believe, that my Dad, wherever he was, would've been proud of the son he created, if only for this one time...then this one time would have to be enough.

©2015

©2015

More Information - silverstreakmedia@gmail.com

©2015

www.ingramcontent.com/pod-product-compliance
Lightning Source LLC
Chambersburg PA
CBHW071453170626
46811CB00007B/2568